TRISTAN

THE FRENCH LIST

TRISTAN

Clarence Boulay

Translated by
Teresa Lavender Fagan

LONDON NEW YORK CALCUTTA

PAP
TAGORE
www.bibliofrance.in

The work is published with the support of the
Publication Assistance Programmes of the Institut français

Seagull Books, 2021

Originally published in French by Sabine Wespieser Éditeur, 2018
© Sabine Wespieser Éditeur, 2018

English translation © Teresa Lavender Fagan, 2021

ISBN   978 0 8574 2 881 3

British Library Cataloguing-in-Publication Data
A catalogue record for this book is available from the British Library.

Typeset by Seagull Books, Calcutta, India
Printed and bound in the USA by Integrated Books International

To Anaïs, to Yves
and to my sprite, Viviane

~

To Tristan—the island, the child

~

To Piere
to one day brave time and defy space

What's the good of a party when
you can't hear the roar of the sea?

—*Arne Falk-Rønne*

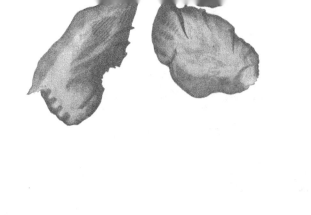

I would have preferred a different story. A story that didn't include me. I would have chosen a more diffuse light. I would have welcomed a god to guide me, in whose footsteps I might have followed. On that peaceful walk I would have eagerly been enchanted by the lovely landscapes, I would have greeted the friendly people, I would have lived, eaten, sung without obstacles or difficulty, been spared the bitterness that still sticks to each of my teeth.

I would have liked to write of a different past. A past that wouldn't cause me to automatically lower my eyes at the question:

So? How was your trip—was it good?

I don't know.

But I can't say that, one doesn't say that.

And so I say, oh, very interesting, and I tell about things that I've told so often that I no longer know if they are fiction or reality.

But I tell.

Probably so I won't disappoint the person who clearly expects me to describe in vivid detail what they've imagined of those months of absence and travel (otherwise, I would be afraid of not living up to the expectations of his or her imagination).

And so, I tell.

A little.

One must make an effort.

1

The foghorn sounds, flooding the ocean. Playful sea lions swim on either side of the boat. Their little cries blending with the groaning of the bumpers that squeal under the pressure of the lobster boat.

Smooth sea, beautiful day, impeccable forecast.

Tears are streaming down my face and I don't even notice. The emotion of the departure, the unadmitted fear of the unknown, the thrill of the waves. Gusts of wind, sobbing, spray, foam, shipwrecks. Unmoored words flood in and spin around in my head, and I can't hold on to any of them. I feel as if the blurry image of the Cape port fading through my tears is being swallowed up inside me, as if this vaporous landscape were now in my stomach. I no longer know. Not really anymore. Shadowy shapes blend with words and echo inside me. I mix up landmarks, lose my bearings, intermittently abandoning my breath to that of the wind. Who, the air or I, is whirling around? My clinched hands grip the salty guardrail as if I'm holding onto the last anchor, holding onto a bit of the mainland to assure myself that I'm not floating away, not entirely, yet.

In front of me, sailors and fishermen, sailing off to work for several months, form a coagulated swarm at the end of the poop deck. Their eyes form a single gaze focusing on the foothills of Table Mountain, which they will see again only upon their return.

Gradually, the horizon swallows up the coast. Robben Island appears, then vanishes. Gradually, the frenzy of the departure gives way to contemplation of the voyage, of what it promises in open sea and birds. So many beautiful birds! Why do departures make everything seem so beautiful?

I'd like to stay just like this, open the parenthesis, settle for life, swallow the spray and the warm air, all the warm air, and swell, swell until I become a sail. I'd like to marry the sea and have the sun as a witness. And the boat continues and I gorge on the air and I want only that.

My cabin is as large as a tiny bathroom. Two superimposed bunk beds, a mattress, a tiny table. Mirror, sink, porthole. A cupboard, too, for my personal things. A thin metal bar encircles every piece of furniture to prevent objects from falling during the voyage. Everything is coated with a thin layer of shiny salt that sticks to your fingers when you touch it. On the boat, nothing distinguishes the officers from the sailors: they all wear blue work clothes, except, perhaps, the captain and Santana. The short, stocky body of the young lieutenant is wrapped in an orange jumpsuit, like those worn by construction workers. Actually, the boat itself is a true worksite. It's amazing to see the fishermen repair the traps. They pick them up and turn them around with a finger as if they were weightless, as if they weighed nothing, as if they didn't exist. Their hands are like glistening snakes that weave smoothly through the mesh of the nets. In constant motion, the spools of green string go in and out on each side of a tear. Then three men form a human chain. The first, standing on the deck, takes a repaired trap and hands it to another fisherman who, mysteriously attached to the stack, puts the load on his head and hands it to a sailor standing on the top. As the day progresses, the traps pile up and ultimately form a huge, bottle-green tower. It's tall, it's big, but, the ultimate magic, everything is hanging in the air as if suspended from the sky. Then, as the sun returns to the sea, the deck is emptied of the dozens of fishermen. The anthill of men in blue is replaced by the huge sculpture that reigns in the middle of the deck. Its shadow stretches out to the sea that flows on either side of the *Austral.*

There are twelve passengers on board: Finn, Meg, Robby and Mary, all residents and born on the island, Phil, the director of the school, six South African engineers, commissioned to repair the pier, and myself. We all gather during meals in the little passenger dining room.

Even before sitting down, Robby puts a plastic bottle of water on the table.

'It's volcano water,' he tells us proudly. 'When I go to the mainland, I take several litres with me. This is the last bottle left—I kept it just for the return.'

Once the plates of food are served, no one says a word. The passengers concentrate on their plates, watching them vigilantly. They scrape their soup and yoghurt bowls until they're immaculate. I watch them, an outsider. What does a meal mean to them?

On the deck, gusts of cold and bracing wind. For a bit of fun, I stretch out my arm and connect the reflection of the moon to the tip of my cigarette which burns Fast with a capital F. I bring the incandescent stick to my mouth and imagine that I'm inhaling a smoke that tastes more celestial and sulphurous. I stay there for a long time, my eyes prisoners of the monochrome expanse before me.

As I'm heading to my cabin, Santana, the second in command, with a quick gesture invites me to join him on the bridge. Along with the young Cuban officer is the helmsman, a tall man with a round stomach, his nose glued to the windshield, his unwavering eyes watching the open sea. All is calm. Only a bip-bip, scarcely audible, escapes from the heady semidarkness.

The glow from the radar screens reveals the young lieutenant's dark skin and black eyes, over which hang heavy, bushy eyebrows. Santana glances at the anemometer illuminated by a nightlight, and breaks the silence with some small talk:

'We're lucky with the weather. It's not always like this. It's supposed to hold until we get there.'

Then the lieutenant is silent for a long time.

'Two years ago, a woman from the island went to the mainland to have her baby. On the way back, the weather was so bad, we were tossed in all directions by an 8-metre swell.

Everyone was throwing up their guts, even the captain, to give you an idea! When we were close to the island, the sea was so choppy that they couldn't disembark the passengers. I don't know if they told you, but there isn't a deep-water port on the island, so everything is unloaded offshore. For a week, we kept turning around that cursed rock to stay in the zone sheltered from the wind. The problem was that the woman had run out of milk for her baby, and she couldn't nurse it. It was up to Jake, the island's policeman, not us, to arrange a dinghy. But the thing was, he considered the conditions too dangerous to disembark the woman and her baby. After ten days at sea, the mother had to give her baby water.'

Santana then pulls his eyes from the sea and plants them in mine.

'Finally, a dinghy came to evacuate them. That time, it really was a close call! And even so, we were lucky, sometimes you make the journey for nothing: the weather is so bad that, when you arrive, you have to go back without unloading anything. Yes, there's a helicopter landing pad on the island, but there's no pilot. It would cost a fortune to keep a pilot and a chopper on the island year-round!'

And, with a strained smile, the young officer adds:

'But, you'll see, over there it's really peaceful. There's no theft, no violence, it's like a little village, except that the nearest coast is a seven-day journey by boat.'

Then nothing more, Santana's Spanish ceases.

After breakfast, Finn settles down on one of the faded leatherette benches in the dining room to do his homework. Little bunches of red pimples are sprouting on the teenager's face, like lighted Christmas-tree decorations. Mary, overseeing his work, is looking over the young man's notebook. Then the woman with an ageless face slowly raises her head until her eyes meet mine.

'The island is looking for a school on the mainland for students who want to continue their studies,' she tells me, as if to interrupt our mute encounter that is visibly making her uncomfortable.

'For the time being, there isn't a partnership yet. On the island, school only goes until students are fifteen, then they start an apprenticeship either in various sectors of the admin- istration or at the cannery, it's their choice.'

I watch her speak. Her soft and silky voice contrasts with the stiffness of her face.

'We have partnerships with Saint Helena, the Falklands, the Isle of Man and Ascension,' she continues. 'As for me, to become a teacher, I lived for a year in Jamestown. Finn is going to be fifteen in July. He's the next student to leave school, that's why he made the trip.'

When the homework is done, the teacher and her student join the other passengers on the bridge. Meg is staring at the GPS. After being gone for several weeks, everyone is extremely eager to get back, especially Meg, who left her husband and children on the island to help Mary and Phil choose a partner school.

That evening, Santana doesn't need to invite me. When he sees me, I understand he was expecting me.

'I hope I didn't scare you last night with the story of the woman and her baby. You mustn't worry. The weather is on our side, it's nothing like what we went through that time. We should even gain a half-day. Are you staying on the island for a while?'

I realize that this is the first question anyone has asked me since we set off.

'Three and a half months. I'm expected on the June boat for the return. The administrator's secretary wrote that I should be able to get on it.'

My Portuguese is bad, but it's the only language that comes out of my mouth in response to Santana's Spanish.

'I must warn you, the number of spots on board is the least certain thing on this earth! All it takes is an emergency hospitalization, a simple medical need or an urgent delivery for you to be bumped to the next boat.'

'And when is that one?'

'I don't know. Sometimes there are two in two weeks, sometimes three months can go by without anyone leaving. They should have the dates at the administrator's office. But, it's really not that complicated, there are only three boats that go to the island: us, the *Meridian* and the *Spire*. The *Spire* belongs to the South African government. It shows up only once a year on a set date to bring the dentist and the ophthalmologist. South Africa has a deal with the island. The island allows South Africa to leave a team of six climatologists on

Bath, a tiny little rock located a day's journey by sea south of the archipelago. In exchange, the boat goes to the island. So, we coordinate with the *Spire*, knowing that apart from the docs it holds only cargo. We carry goods and passengers to the island, then we go fishing for two months in the area near the rock in question. Why are you going to the island?'

This evening, I would like to release all words, be rid of them, confer them to the wind. This evening, I have no desire to speak. Keep only the night and voices. Especially voices, all the voices. Do nothing but listen. Even so, doing is too much. A desire for a human jukebox that would recite endless stories for hours and years. Stories. Even true ones. I simply say to him:

'*Faz favor Santana, conta-me histórias.*'

And Santana begins. That evening, there's no need to go anywhere. Going is enough.

Friday, 4 March, second day at sea
Sorry it's taken me so long to write, Léon. The few days spent on the Cape before setting off were pretty difficult. Everything was stolen: my passport, my camera and the key to my room— I don't know how it happened. But the embassy sent me an emergency passport.

Here, on board, the days are long, but also short. I don't really know anymore. The passengers from the island are particularly kind to me. I'm having trouble with this, because even if the swell is weak, writing makes me seasick.

I'll return to my note soon.
Ida

This morning, the sea is calm, the sun floods over us, there are fewer and fewer birds, just a scattering of seabirds persist in the lobster boat's wake. During the day, Phil, the teacher and director of the school, sits down with me on the upper deck. We take canvas deck chairs out of huge cabinets where the supplies are stored, and read in the shadow of the tall smoke-stack.

I begin to read the annals of Professor Faustini, in which the Italian geographer, a specialist of Polar regions, lists the events that have marked the island since it was discovered. The first page of the book is peppered with tiny dots that look like pin pricks. In the middle of the swarm there is a circle, scarcely larger than the little dots that surround it. At the bottom of the page the legend says: *Map of shipwrecks off the coast of the island from 1811 to 1925.*

'You know, the history of the island is a story of its shipwrecks.'

Phil's serious voice makes me jump. The teacher, who must have recognized the book's cover, folds his newspaper and lays it on his sunburnt knees.

'Without them, I think it would still be uninhabited. The island is the only inhabited place on this part of the globe. It takes only a malfunction on board, the implosion of a motor, the dismasting of a sailboat, or for any type of accident to occur between Africa and America, for boats to stop there and for the residents to mobilize. Emergency situations are the stuff of their everyday lives. It is rare for a month to go by without a siren going off or a request for assistance being sounded. Imagine, the island is the only inhabited landmark in a maritime perimeter that is three times the size of the United States!'

At that moment, the captain and Jack, the navigation officer, cross the deck in the direction of the intermediate platform.

'Ben, the captain, is a former poacher,' Phil whispers to me. 'In the 90s, he fished for lobster in the northern waters between Saint Paul Island and the Kerguelen Islands, until he was caught by the French. It could have cost him dearly, but, from what they say, he got out of it without too much trouble. Since then, the *Austral* is pretty much his hideout. You know, I make this trip pretty frequently. I know the crew as well as I do the inhabitants of the island. I've been living there with my wife almost fourteen years. In the beginning, not really knowing what to expect, I had signed a three-year contract, but I decided to extend it when the contract was up.'

Phil stops talking and beckons to Jack, who stops for a moment with us.

'So, I see there are some new sailors on board. Did you change crews?'

'Yeah, during the last trip, we barely avoided a catastrophe: we were only about halfway when the sailors began to get mad because they thought they weren't paid enough. Gradually, the situation got worse and, after a few days, half the fishermen refused to work. It's always like that: it only takes one or two hot heads to stir the pot and for everyone to follow them. Then there was such a shit show that we had to turn back. What do you think we can do on a lobster boat, except fish? It's true, we work under difficult conditions, but you can't do anything about it, and it's not our fault if the fishermen are paid badly. It's the company that pays the salaries, not us! And so, most of the fishermen went somewhere else, and the company was forced to recruit. But the problem is that with men who have less training, you catch fewer lobsters, also, newbies think it's a great life, but once you've set off, its constantly *catch, catch, catch, catch.*'

While he's talking, Jack hoists an imaginary net, bringing his hands together, then he pauses, winded by the exertion of his mime. He leans his elbows on the rusty railing and lets his head fall between his bulging biceps.

'Lobsters are my entire life. Did you see all the traps piled up on the deck? Well, I'm the one who soldered them, one by one. I built a workshop in front of my house in Papendorp, near Cape Town.'

Jack is silent a moment, then continues.

'If you want, tomorrow, I can show you the packing room.'

Phil and I nod enthusiastically. The lieutenant raises his head.

'Great, that will work, tomorrow, we'll visit the slaughterhouse.'

Then he disappears, like a current of air.

Indifferent to hours meant for sleeping, I listen to Santana, my evening radio. Tonight, the young officer invites me to Cuba. He tells me about women, his wife, his father, crushed by a farm machine last July, he tells me about himself and above all about the sea. In his mouth, the words burn and are consumed, fusing in mass against the invisible walls of the passageway. Next to us, standing behind the large wheel bar, the helmsman remains motionless. Towards what secret places do his thoughts wander during these silent nights? Maybe Santana speaks in Spanish so he won't be understood by him. After a long moment, the young Cuban concedes: 'Being a sailor is one of the only ways to leave that *bloody country*. In any case, the moment you set foot on board, it's over, you will never again feel like those who remain. There are landlubbers and there are the others, who will always feel foreign. To embark is necessarily to be at a distance, to follow a tangent. After a time, you end up no longer recognizing land except as a coastline.'

In front of us, the reflection of the moon, our only beacon, illuminates the heavy and opaque expanse that nevertheless seems transparent to the officer's eyes.

Saturday, 5 March, third day at sea.
I'm more focused today, Léon. Outside, the blue floods in over and over at every instant.

My feet are scorched by the sun, but I'm getting used to it.

How are you? It's constant torture knowing you're so far away.

The packing room is a true onboard factory, filled entirely with stainless steel. Dozens of tools of indescribable shapes are hung along the walls on large metal hooks. Jack walks by each station and begins his lesson:

'Once the lobsters are caught in the traps, the men dump them into these large aluminium chutes that go from the upper deck to here. The smallest catches are measured with a calliper, and if the tail is less than 8 centimetres they're thrown back into the sea. With the bigger ones, the guys cut off the tails before putting the heads in this vat, so they can be crushed and poured back into the ocean. The tails are then placed on screens and cooked in these ovens, then they're wrapped and frozen in the cold chamber.'

Jack turns some handles, opens the doors to the ovens, slides open the door of the cold chamber. With these movements, the entire packing room is set in motion; I can imagine the shellfish descending by the hundreds down the chutes, their abdomens arched, piling up in the huge stainless steel vats, the scalding platters coming out of the ovens, filled with lobster tails reddened by the heat. We see the men in action, measuring, sorting, counting, crushing, cooking, packing and transporting the shellfish. Jack turns around and looks at us, clearly proud of his domain.

'During fishing season, the packing room is open 24/7, and we work in shifts, like on the bridge.'

Before we return to the upper deck, the lieutenant takes us through the fishermen's quarters. A diffuse mixture of R&B, pop, and kizomba comes out of the cabins whose doors are for the most part missing. Inside the rooms, mountains of blue work clothes and safety shoes are piled next to sports magazines and photos of naked women. Three or four sailors share the same cabin. Most of them are stretched out on their bunks. They smoke cigarettes, tap on their cell phones, play cards. Wafting out of one of the cabins, there is an odour of food frying on a little hot plate balanced on a tiny sink. A fisherman is frying something he probably caught in the boat's wake. While the fish is frying, another sailor comes out of the shower, a towel around his hips, and goes into his cabin. Even if no one seems annoyed by our visit, I feel I'm intruding. Jack must sense my discomfort, because he gestures for us to follow him.

Back on the upper deck, Phil and I return to our chairs and our respective reading. For three centuries, from 1509 to 1810, the island appeared on maps, though no one ever settled there permanently. In 1816, the English officially annexed the archipelago: the island is the territory closest to St Helena, and the English wanted to ensure that their French enemies wouldn't use the islands as a base from which to free Napoleon Bonaparte. A year later, the English squadron left the island. The evacuation turned into a disaster. The ship that had been mobilized for the move was wrecked. Fifty-five men perished at sea. During the island's demilitarization, the head corporal requested authorization to remain there with his wife, his two children and two masons, and they began to build the foundations of a community, facing epidemics, famines, shipwrecks and the exiled which, since that time, have never stopped arriving.

Morning, noon, evening; get up, deck, sun, bridge, bed. The succession of days gradually settles into a rhythm. The passengers are increasingly impatient. They all have their eyes riveted on the GPS in the wheel room where they now stay all day long.

This morning, there are no more birds with us. Now there's nothing to catch one's eye, nothing to distract; no profile out at sea, no boat in sight. The days go by and the space begins again. Sea, day, blue. Day, sea, blue. Monochrome variations that endow one's gaze with the tactile acuity of a blind person. Little by little I feel I am being freed of a weight, liberated from a heaviness, as if my skin is being shed during the voyage. Around me, strips of the past flutter in the wind, revealing a new skin, fresh, filled with possibilities that I sense are rising on the horizon.

Monday, 7 March, fifth day at sea.
I'm floating, Léon. I'm floating. How can I place the words to describe this crazy impression? Everything is unravelling, but I'm not afraid.

Who called me? I heard a voice. Who called out? I look out the porthole. Outside, the same unchanging expanse is floating in front of me. In the dining room, the passengers are at the table, each faithfully sitting at the place they chose on the first day. Three of the six South African engineers are missing; sick as dogs, they're lying prostrate in their cabins.

I sit down among the passengers.

'Did anyone hear the noise this morning, like voices, shouts?'

The passengers look at me, unfocused.

'Sharp voices, piercing, really, they seemed to be coming from the deck.'

No one says a thing. Then, suddenly, Robby bursts out laughing.

'Molly, molly, I'm sure she heard a molly!'

Robby's amused response is now echoed by everyone else. The dining room trembles with the synergetic laughter of my fellow passengers. I look at them, an outsider.

'It's not voices,' Phil explains, 'it's the albatrosses. On the island, they're called "mollies". The "mollies" arrived during the night, it's a sign we're getting close to shore.'

On the deck there's the most joyful party I've ever attended. They are everywhere, long, white, immaculate, waltzing languorously above the lobster boat with infinite poise. Their wide glistening wings slice through the air with a dry, self-assured rustling. Then, the albatrosses leave us and fly straight ahead, as if to show the shift lieutenant the way, and then they suddenly surge up before us again. My eyes are huge marbles glued to the sky, fascinated by the enchanting ballet. The five passengers watch the stage, amused by my adoring innocence.

A few hours later, Jack bursts into my cabin.

'Hey, do you want to see how we fish for birds?'

His question is intriguing. I imagine big, flying fish in the sky.

'Come on, we're going to fish for your supper!'

I follow the lieutenant with the military bearing along the corridor. We arrive on the lower deck, at the place where the boat forms its wide wake. Behind us, three sailors, lying on a pile of mooring lines, are passing around a bottle of whiskey. Jack puts the head of a fish onto a large hook.

'Go ahead,' he says to me, 'throw out the line, but be careful of your feet.'

I throw out the bait and the thick transparent line flies off in a shot. Dozens of metres of filament in only a few seconds disappear into the churn of the waves regurgitated by the sea behind the moving boat. Once unrolled, the line is stretched and disappears on the water's surface. At that moment, two huge albatrosses appear. With a snap of its beak, one of them bites the hook, lets out a piercing cry and convulses before giving up completely, pulled by the taut cord. Jack looks at me and smiles before quickly reeling in the catch. I turn around and race down the corridor.

That evening, for the first time, tongues are untied during the meal. There is an urgency, a haste in the voices. Meg can't stop talking about her dog, Woolfy. Robby wonders out loud how fishing on the island has been while he was away. The South African engineers have obviously made an effort to leave their cabins and join us in the dining room. Some of them seem to have lost a few kilos during the trip. Mary laughs for no real reason, it's odd, almost touching, to see the joy on her face.

I watch them, pensive. For the first time, I sense we have formed a little community, like a patchwork quilt that was sewn together during the voyage.

'By the way, do you know who you'll be staying with?' Meg asks me.

'No, I have no idea. The administrator's secretary didn't tell me.'

'I heard you're going to stay with my younger brother and his wife. If that's true, you'll be fine there. You'll see, Mike and Vera are lovely people,' she says with the general agreement of the other passengers. 'Their house is above the village. It overlooks the community.'

Robby gets up, puts on his glasses and walks over to a plastic-covered photo hanging on one of the dining-room walls. The shot, taken from a plane, is of a narrow plateau situated between the ocean and the walls of a huge volcano. A number of houses with multicoloured roofs are scattered everywhere over the green expanse that plunges into the sea. The houses seem microscopic compared to the slopes of the volcano.

'Mike lives there,' says Robby, putting the end of the earpiece of his glasses on a tiny red spot at the foot of a bluff.

This evening, Santana is quiet. This evening, I don't depart with him. Not to Cuba, or anywhere else. I don't meet his wife or head off on the boats that he has navigated over oceans in every direction. This evening, there is no sea to talk about, there is only the clearing of the throat of the helmsman who must have caught a cold. I stay seated, deep in the captain's chair, my gaze lost in the starry vault of the radar screens.

Tuesday, 8 March, sixth day at sea.
*I feel as if I've settled into the voyage the way one settles into
an overstuffed armchair. And yet, Léon, tomorrow, we arrive,
tomorrow, there will be land. It's incredible to write that.*

Five in the morning. Longitude, latitude. I see the spark in the
distance. A light, after seven days at sea, that attracts one's
gaze, that attaches itself to one's eyes. *In the ocean, a glint, an
island.*

The island, the way it surges up, could have been parachuted down right then, right in front of us, just for us. Why
an island? Why a volcano here? Why land and not nothing?
And yet, the island is indeed there, and the volcano rises up,
majestic, imposing.

On the deck, the passengers and the fishermen form a
crowd huddled in the front of the boat. Robby is wearing a
bright pink shirt with a huge, roaring lion that is stretched
over his protruding stomach. Mary has put on eye make-up
and is wearing discreet, softly dangling earrings. Meg has
exchanged her sneakers for a pair of pumps, and Finn has
put gel in his hair in a battle against the wind. As for me, I'm
still wearing my old jeans and fleece top, unaware of any
dressing-up ritual.

Everything happens very quickly; scarcely has the boat
moored when two barges arrive, piloted by men in fishing gear
and red raincoats. A dozen men climb on board the lobster
boat. Meg runs to one of them, takes him in her arms and
won't let him go. Then Mary, Meg, Phil, Finn and I find a place
in a tiny blue wooden container that the crane of the *Austral*

places on one of the two barges floating a few meters below. The space is so tiny that I have to sit on Meg's lap.

'We're really lucky,' she tells me. 'The last time, just as they were setting the container on the barge, there was a gust of wind and we started to fly around in every direction, we hit the hull of the *Austral* twice. It was horrible.'

When we arrive a few minutes later, the port is thronged. In front of us, dozens of people are lined up, impatiently waiting their turn to greet the new arrivals, to offer them gifts. Some hug and kiss, women shed a few tears, others shake hands, but always a bit shyly.

A short, roundish woman, smiling, greets me amid the overall hubbub. '*Are you Ida?*' I nod yes as warmly as possible. Without hesitation, the young woman holds out her hand and then introduces me to a slim, blond, also smiling woman.

'This is Vera, you'll be staying at her place while you're with us.' I shake this young woman's hand, and without further niceties, she invites me to follow her.

We cross through the village and leave behind the joyful animation flowing from the port. I look at the colours, the light, the life that is unfolding around me: the flowers, the dogs, the chickens, the little roads and the charming houses. Vera's is the last, at the very top of the village. Before going through the door, I turn around. In front of me, the landscape is long and blue.

I don't know a soul on the island, no one is expecting me. The page is blank. Anything is possible. No. Everything seems possible. But I only find that out later.

2

I sit down on the duvet and stay there a long time looking around the room. The lamp, the mirror, the fake-wood armoire, the little stuffed animal sitting on the armchair; everything seems incredibly fixed to me, like figurines in a wax museum. The droning of the boat's motor is still echoing in my head and fills the room.

Vera's transparent face appears in the open door. She is smiling.

'I have to leave. On the days when the ships unload, there's a lot of work at the shop. If you need anything, you can knock on Betty's door. It's the first house on the left.'

I nod, then burrow beneath the covers before falling asleep, rocked by the swaying of the boat that I haven't left.

When I wake up, everything is dark. I slip on my shoes and leave my room, guided by Vera's voice coming from the other end of the hallway.

'The little fellow is really unlucky. Last year, too, the boat arrived on his birthday. With the unloading, we all arrived late. Do you remember?'

Sitting at the counter in her large kitchen, Vera is chatting with her husband, a forty-something man, muscular and a bit ungainly. I stay where I am and watch them from the frame of the door. Their gestures, their looks, the inflection of their voices. They are both handsome, one can sense they are joined by a strong, rare connection.

When he notices me, the man's face changes, as if he has suddenly remembered he is shy. He walks slowly towards me and holds out a hesitant hand.

'We haven't been around much today—you have to work fast when the boat arrives because, with the wind, you never know if you'll be able to unload more the next day,' he says to me, in a stiffly assured tone.

'We're going to my nephew Joe's birthday party. Do you want to come with us?' Vera asks me.

I say yes, and smile, still a bit fuzzy from sleep.

We stroll along the heights of the village, guided by the torch beam that shimmers over the cracks in the asphalt. There isn't the rustling of a tree, not a sound, no bit of wind. Around us, the houses are like sleeping shadows. I feel both heavy and incredibly light, carried along by my legs that wobble and sink into the macadam as if it were a carpet of moss. After we walk a few minutes, we arrive in front of a well-kept house with a blue roof. The couple slows down, and Mike turns off the torch. A young woman opens the door and invites us in.

We go into a large room where a small group of women are knitting, sitting around an impressive buffet of food that spreads out, spilling even into the sink. Mike says hello to everyone, then goes off to join the men in the sitting room. Two fat women whose faces are covered with rosacea hold out a stool for me and kindly invite me to sit. I stand there, motionless, like a well-disciplined child worried about behaving in front of the adults, who I gradually sense are all watching me. And I observe, I listen to the scattered conversations, paused by long silences that highlight the movements of the women and the clicking of the knitting needles, the plunging necklines hidden beneath raincoats, dozens of birthday cards scattered around pies, cobblers, meatballs, kabobs, lobster tails and cakes that make up the buffet. It's odd to find myself standing in front of such abundance after the very long and spare voyage.

9 March
Sea, island, house, faces, birthday. I feel as if I've lived five days in one, Léon.

But this evening, I'm happy to be here, to have finally arrived, to have reached this place, this tiny island, that, together, we studied on the map.

It takes me a long moment to recognize the room, locate the objects; the stuffed elephant sitting on the armchair, the purple lace of the curtains, the bedside lamp. It's curious, it could be a child's room.

I get up, get dressed, and go to the kitchen. A note, written in the handwriting of a teenager, is waiting for me on the table.

Your breakfast is in the refrigerator. See you this evening. V. I smile, touched by Vera's kindness, then I fix some tea and decide to go down to the village.

A dirt path winds between small parcels of land and clumps of succulents. Laundry flutters, swelled by the wind, intermittently shadowing the harsh white of the facades and the low basalt walls that surround the houses. As I walk, I feel as if I'm entering into a fairy tale, walking through a drawing, as if everything that surrounds me is both quite real and completely make-believe.

On the way, a woman, followed by a tiny, black dog, stops as we meet.

'Lovely day, isn't it? A south-southeast wind, perfect day for fishing, the men must be happy. We've been waiting for this for a long time!'

I politely agree, completely ignorant of what makes for a good fishing day.

'So, from what I've heard, your boyfriend wasn't able to come?'

I look at the woman, surprised she knows so much.

'Yes, that's right, the administrator's secretary called us the day before our departure to say there was only one place left on board. So we tossed a coin, and I won.' I said in a rush of words.

'Oh, yes! That's not the first time that's happened! With all the storms we've been having, we need a lot of manpower to repair the pier, so, of course, not a lot of places are left on board. But don't worry, your man will be here soon. In two months, the *Meridian* will arrive. And, you know, single men are not in short supply here.'

The woman gives me a knowing look, and walks off, calling her dog. I stand where I am, on the path, incredulous.

Don't worry, Léon, we'll find a frequency, a star, a way to tame the distance. I'm talking to you softly with my own words that are gradually drowning in my exile's tears. How many times have I played the scene over, rewritten the script? If, at that second, the air had been thicker, the coin tossed higher? What if it had fallen on tails? You would be here, Léon, instead of me, you would see the cows grazing and the little whale spinning around on top of the church steeple.

A hundred or so metres farther, the path ends in front of an imposing grey building which shields a large promontory and unveils a magnificent view of the port, humming with activity. A large motorized platform is moving between the dock and the *Austral* which is anchored a short distance away, while a dozen dinghies, filled with crates loaded with lobsters, slowly come into the mouth of the port. Standing on the bow, I recognize Mike, Vera's husband, who is tying up his boat, weaving between the traps and the nets piled up on the deck. His slightly ungainly body here shows incredible deftness and agility. The hand that lands on my shoulder makes me jump.

'I called the house, but no one answered. I just wanted to tell you that I'll be back later than normal this evening. On fishing days, work picks up at the cannery. There is some stuffed mutton in the oven. You just have to heat it up. Will that be OK?'

I nod, and watch Vera walk away and join the women who descend from the heights of the village and, like little ants, go into the cannery.

Back at the house, I put on my running clothes. I need to run, to find my legs again. I take the concrete path and let myself be guided by the route that winds in and out among the hills. Gradually, the relief flattens out and gives way to a vast expanse of land divided up into countless parcels. I slow my pace and stop, captivated by the power that emerges from the landscape. And yet, there's nothing spectacular: the slopes of the volcano, the ocean, the green of the hills and the silence, deafening.

Léon,

Where are your arms? Where is the body that I steal from the night and which completes me? Two months, the woman told me. In two months, you'll be here.

Mike set up a large table in the sitting room for me, looking out at the sea. Every morning, I watch the ocean before I sit down at the table to write and draw, until lunchtime. But today, while looking out the window, it seems that something has changed; as if the landscape has broken, lost its balance. Something has disappeared, vanished, but what?

The *Austral* is gone. The boat isn't there anymore. The ocean suddenly seems incredibly empty and enormous.

I put down my notebook, my pencils, and run down the path to the Internet cafe. I need to write to you, to reassure myself that you're still there. The little white building, scarcely bigger than a garage, is flying a Union Jack framed by two golden lobsters with a sailboat above them. A woman is trying desperately to shut the front door which bangs open with each gust of wind.

I say hello, and sit in front of the screen she directs me to. And I begin to write. Waves, the wind, my arrival on the island, Vera, Mike, and the distance that, now that I've arrived, I feel is growing greater.

After a while, the woman's stare becomes insistent.

'You went running the other day, in the patches,' says the tall brunette, smiling widely.

'Yes, but that's odd, I don't think I saw anyone.'

'You went as far as Big Molly Gulch and you came back,' she says, still smiling, before glancing outdoors. 'Not bad for a run.'

I smile in turn, uneasy at knowing that people have been observing me so closely, then get back to my message. But I scarcely have time to write a few lines when the woman interrupts me again.

'It's closing time. I have to lock up. They're expecting me at the cannery. Can you come back tomorrow?'

I say yes, disappointed that I can't write more, and go back to the house.

Around me, Léon, there are people, pretty much all the same, dogs, pretty much all the same, houses, too, all the same. Why does everything look alike when you arrive somewhere? Why is there that feeling, very odd, that everything is the same?

The door creaks. The worshippers turn around. We're late. Vera goes down the aisle, her head bowed. Mike hands me a missal and a Bible, and motions for me to follow them. Under her long robe, I recognize the woman from the Internet cafe. Her robe of immaculate white contrasts with the dark mass of the faithful whom I can only see from the back. Around me, I catch the glances that escape discreetly from the pews to land on me, unlike those of the children who boldly break the rules of etiquette and openly turn around. *Lord, have mercy, Lord, have mercy, Christ, have mercy, Christ, have mercy.* During each prayer, Vera conscientiously passes her finger over the missal to help me follow. I suddenly feel invested with a role that is not my own: I have become the child they are protecting, the one they probably pray for every Sunday, and which they still don't have. I suddenly want to run away, to leave, to run through the door to find the air that I desperately need. Why did I agree to go to services with them? *Blessed be God forever, God bless you. Amen.* The Eucharist finally ends. I rush to the exit, relieved to feel the wind sweeping across my face and scattering my thoughts. The congregation slowly moves outside and disperses into the village.

Back at the house, we prepare breakfast together. I need to eat, to regain my strength. Gradually, the table is transformed into a vast palette filled with colours, covered with fried eggs—both chicken and duck—bacon, sausages, margarine, cheddar cheese, baked beans, tea and toast. 'You have to cleanse your soul before satisfying the body,' Mike says to me, smiling, obviously just as impatient as I am to sit down.

Today, Léon, after church, I asked Mike and Vera if I could go with them in the mornings to milk the cows. Mike seemed surprised, even amused. 'You know, there's nothing extra-ordinary, we go to the field, Vera milks Suzy, and we come back.' Then he looked at his wife, as if he regretted speaking too quickly. Vera didn't say anything. She just smiled. 'You can come if you want. After all, that's how you learn,' she finally said. I looked at them and smiled. I'm happy I can go with them.

The following day, Vera opens the gate and starts walking up the path quickly. But it's not her usual time. I hear her walk around the house, opening cupboard doors and banging them shut again. 'Toilet paper, pants, raincoat, flashlight, headlamp, matches, T-shirt, knife, sleeping bag, bread, beer, sherry, brandy,' she recites like a nursery rhyme as she goes through the rooms.

Mike gets out of a pick-up truck and comes into the house only to leave again a few minutes later, carrying two large canvas bags and a life vest. Vera follows behind him and takes the path that goes down to the village. Then, nothing else; the tick-tock of the clock and the snoring of the dogs. I decide to turn that flash of light into a mirage, and go back to my watercolour; there are fishing boats lined up along the dock. Long streaks of rain, which surprised me while I was drawing, run down the hulls as if the boats were melting. It makes them more unusual, a bit mysterious. I like it.

A few hours later, back from work, Vera turns on the VHF radio and begins ironing. A man in his fifties, his face sprinkled with freckles, comes into the room and silently sits down at the kitchen counter.

'Hi, Tony,' Vera greets him, without raising her head. The man doesn't move for a moment and lets his eyes wander around the room.

'It seems the commander has a huge black eye. He must have been hit right in the face. Poor guy, I wouldn't like to have been in his shoes. I hope no one else got hurt, otherwise, they'll soon be overwhelmed at the hospital,' he says, turning towards Vera.

I come into the room, intrigued by the conversation. Vera sets down the iron and serves us all a glass of brandy.

'Sometime during the night, a 200-metre cargo boat carrying thousands of tonnes of soy beans ran aground off Bird Island, 20 miles from here, and is dumping oil. No one lives there, but it's one of the main places where penguins mate. This afternoon, Mike went over there with a dozen other men to begin collecting the animals while they wait for clean-up crews to arrive from the mainland,' she explains to me, seeming preoccupied.

Tony nods in agreement before continuing, clearly angry:

'It's not really complicated, is it? There are three rocks in the entire ocean and the guy had to go and hit one. I'm sorry, but I don't call that a sailor!'

Vera gestures him to be quiet and turns up the volume of the VHF hanging above the gas stove.

'*Prince Albert, Prince Albert for Island radio, do you copy? Over.*'

After a bit of crackling, the radio resumes.

'*Island radio, Island radio, for Prince Albert, go ahead.*'

'Hello, commander Mayer, we're going to anchor 2 miles offshore for the night. Passenger excursion expected at 10 a.m. Do you confirm?'

'Yes, we confirm. Do . . . '

The VHF is suddenly silent.

'Damn, the battery's dead. And, of course, I forgot the charger at the shop.'

'If I were you, I'd ask Jake if you could go take a look,' Tony says to me.

'To see the ship?'

'Yeah, I went once to see a cruise ship, a few years ago, and I can tell you it's well worth it. Tomorrow, go see Jake, the island policeman. He's the one who directs comings and goings, he's responsible for immigration and Customs, ask him to ask the captain to give you a little tour!'

Tony gives me a wink, then leaves, without saying anything else. Just then, a heavy woman, followed by a little black dog, knocks on the door and greets us. I recognize the woman whom I ran into on the path to the village shortly after I arrived. She sits down on the sofa and doesn't say anything, trying to catch her breath.

'Did you hear? Tomorrow, the *Prince Albert* is going to make a stop here. With the shipwreck last night, it's really not the best time, to say the least!'

'Oh, you know, it's always like that, Dora. It's calm for months, then, all of a sudden, our heads are spinning!' Vera responds, refilling our glasses with brandy.

'From what I've heard, the administrator asked for reinforcements from South Africa to get men and materiel to limit the spread of the oil.'

'We'll see,' says Vera, pensively. 'It seems a lot of penguins are already covered in oil.'

We stay there sipping our brandy and looking at the dogs dozing in their basket. It's strange, I have the impression I'm seeing a dog sleep for the first time. Vera turns on the light, pulling me from my thoughts. Dora calls her dog and says goodbye.

17 March

This evening, Léon, I wanted to talk to you, to hear you, to listen to you breathe. To grasp a laugh, a tone, a breath of voice, to really be sure that you still exist.

See you soon, see you asap,

Ida

The passengers of the *Prince Albert* disembarked. Vera, Tony, Fanny, Dora and the others were waiting for them on the pier to show them around the island. The 'guests' first walked around the village, they visited the church, took photos of the whale-shaped weathervane, the school and the Albatross Bar before stopping at the shop to buy sweaters, caps and wool penguins which, all year long, the women knit to sell to the rare visitors passing through. Some tourists then played golf in the cow pasture, next to the weather station where, the day before, I had seen some men placing poles, which looked like hole markers, in rat burrows. Then, before nightfall, the cruise passengers got back on board, en route to Namibia, Angola and São Tomé.

While they were in town, I visited the *Prince Albert*. A major-domo showed me the smoking room, the spa, the royal suites and the teakwood deck. Through the porthole I watched the tourists wind their way between the colourful houses. I watched the cows, the road that leads to the potato patches and the clouds caught at the top of the volcano. Two islands, two worlds, both so close and yet so far apart.

This morning, Léon, I sat down at my work table and was looking out the window. I picked up a pencil and drew a long line from my paper to the sea. A diving board, a tether, or a string that I'm holding out for you to take. Maybe.

It's become a routine; every morning, we carry lamps, buckets and pitchers out to the pasture. Vera and Fanny, her cousin, begin milking while Oliver, Fanny's husband, watches the dogs. I sit on the low wall that surrounds the pasture and I watch, silent. Vera is beautiful. A wild, crystalline beauty, which clashes with the rusticity of the surroundings.

Once the milking is done, Fanny and Oliver invite us over for some tea. Fanny fills her old cast-iron tea kettle with water and allows the whistling of the steam to sound over the crackling of the VHF sitting on the table.

Oliver mechanically stirs the tea bag that is floating on the surface of his cup. He seems preoccupied.

'The hull of the cargo ship broke open. It burst last evening. Right in the middle. You can't imagine the damage it has caused. The administrator asked the insurance company to charter a cargo boat and two towboats. He also ordered electric generators, high-pressure water hoses and all the stuff needed to feed and take care of the oil-covered birds. We still don't know where the currents are going to take the oil. Not to mention that, in the meantime, a ship has to agree to change course to pick up the crew. The poor guys, they can't stay on the island doing nothing! In any case, we can't count on the *Meridian*—the passenger list has been closed for six months!'

'The municipal pool has been requisitioned to hold the oily penguins for the time being, while they wait for the equipment to arrive,' Fanny adds. 'For three days, I went around to all the houses to ask folks if they would agree to house any Filipino crew. I found rooms for everyone except the captain. No one wanted him, so the administrator was forced to get him a room in the hospital, can you imagine?'

While Fanny is talking, Vera is staring at the little tea leaves floating on the surface of her cup. It looks like she is counting them, when, all of a sudden, she looks at her watch and sets down her cup.'

'It's time, Ida, we have to go.'

When we're back at the house, I take my sketchbook and pencils, and go out to draw. Outside, a light, cool wind makes the long stalks of grass and the clumps of flax undulate. An unusual brouhaha can be heard from the outskirts of the village. I get closer, guided by the sound, and discover an unreal sight; hundreds of rockhopper penguins are splashing in the water left at the bottom of the municipal pool, causing a deafening din. Their little white stomachs, their jet-black wings and backs, are covered with a viscous black paste. Some of them are standing motionless, their eyes closed; it seems they are already dead.

I sit down on a rock and watch the scene, dumbstruck, then I take out my sketchbook and begin to draw.

Two men, sitting in the middle of the pool, capture the little animals one by one in an attempt to feed them.

'Are there penguins in France?' one of them asks me.

'No, just in aquariums.'

'Then, take a few with you!'

The fifty-something man smiles, obviously amused by what he said.

'Tell me, my son has been living in England for fifteen years, and he says he's never seen a single penguin. Kilbrey, do you know it? That's where my boy and his wife live.'

'No, I've never been there, but I don't really know the UK very well.'

The man is silent and gets back to work, then stops and looks at me.

'It would be better if you help feed these poor animals instead of just drawing them.'

What he said might have hurt me, but I think it frees me.

'The teams have been formed for today, but tomorrow, come to the hangar at 8 a.m. The administrator's wife will find a job for you; we need as many folks as we can get!' he continues, as if he has noticed the switch that has been turned on by his invitation.

23 March

Thank you for your messages, Léon. Every day, I copy them into my notebook and reread them, in the evening, before going to bed.

Here, the black tide seems to have done a great deal of damage. When the wind allows, men set off for Bird Island and come back at night with loads of penguins covered in oil. Mike hasn't come back yet. He's staying there, with three other men, to capture the birds who will be brought back here.

I love you, Léon,

your arms, your back, your feet.

Some thirty people are waiting silently in front of the old mechanical-department hangar. Mila, the administrator's wife, soon arrives. The short woman, well-dressed and smiling, greets everyone warmly and goes over a list of names written in a notebook. Once the volunteers have their assignments, only I and an old man, with a swarthy face framed by interminable ear lobes flowing from his ears, are left.

'Two people—that will be perfect for collections! Follow me,' Mila instructs us.

'While we wait for reinforcements to arrive, my husband has launched an appeal to the community to contribute fish that will be used to feed the several hundred penguins that have already been brought over,' she explains while we walk. 'Ida, you'll help Andy check them in, OK?'

I agree, happy to be useful.

'You'll station yourselves in the little cabin that is usually used for cutting up fish. You'll see, Andy will explain everything,' says the little blond woman, all smiles, before walking off, obviously very busy.

The space is spartan: two chairs, a table, and a scale hanging from the beam of the room. The old man takes a little black notebook out of his pocket and hands it to me.

'This is for you. You have to write down the names of the people and the weight of the donation. I'll take care of cutting up the fish. OK?'

The man looks at me and smiles. I like the way he talks, the softness of his words. His very unusual face makes me think of an engraving that Léon had hung above his desk. It shows five very dark-skinned women getting out of a large sailboat. Enthralled with the history of the island, Léon had explained to me that, in 1827, the head corporal, who stayed on the island with his family after the evacuation of the English squadron, had asked a sailor passing by to bring back five women from St Helena, the closest inhabited territory, to help populate the community which at the time was made up only of his family and five men, all of whom had essentially been shipwrecked. As soon as they arrived, the five Saints were married, and the couples repopulated the island with mulatto children.

The rumbling of the pick-up that parks in front of the cabin pulls me out of my thoughts. A tall, thirty-something man comes in and sets down onto the tray of the scale two enormous sacks filled with frozen fish. Then Dora, Tony, Fanny, Vera and dozens of other residents of the island show up, and the cabin is quickly filled with a mountain of 'five-fingers' and Cape mackerels that Andy scales, cuts up and chops into small cubes 'big enough but not too big, to be able to put them in their gullets.' I like watching him do it; his way of slowly sharpening his knife, of gutting the fish while looking out the window, both present and a bit elsewhere.

When our work is done, I take a detour by the pool before returning home and going for a run. The penguins continue to cry out, to jump, to slide in the pool, but with less energy. All around them, dead birds are scattered on the ground covered with thick clouds of blue flies. Up above, albatrosses and skuas, drawn by the smell of dead bodies, shriek loudly and circle around in the sky.

26 March

I saw them while I was running, up on the hill. They were all lined up and were following each other single file along the road that leads to the patches. The Filipino crew were swimming in too-large clothing loaned to them by the residents, they are swimming on this island, this rock parachuted into the ocean. They're waiting without waiting for a boat to

change course, still not knowing, Africa or America, which
coast they will see first.

See you soon, my Great Eagle.

Ida

Like every morning this week, we go down to the village after milking the cows. Vera goes to the mini-market and I sit in front of the cabin, opposite the sea, waiting for Andy whose slim figure I can see slowly getting closer, breaking through the first rays of the sun. He greets me with a quick gesture, then places his lunch on the concrete floor of the little room.

And the day starts again. Day after day, we carry out the same functions. The notebook now has more than two hundred names, that is, more than two-thirds of the residents. They have all passed through our little hut to set down their contributions. But, this morning, the cabin is empty: no one comes to bring fish, and we stay the entire morning seated in front of the window, looking out at the ocean.

'Their freezers are empty,' old Andy keeps repeating. 'We just have to wait for help to arrive to feed the penguins.'

He doesn't know his statement would prove to be a premonition: at noon, two boats rise up on the horizon. The news quickly spreads and, in a few minutes, the whole village is running to the port, forming a crowd on the promontory. Scarcely disembarked, the South African crews get to work putting up enclosures, installing washing stations and conduits for a fresh water supply. The next day, the area round the requisitioned hangar looks like a real veterinary clinic. Hundreds of penguins are gathered in crates, separated by net partitions and lighted by ultraviolet lamps. Vera has left her job at the shop for the time being, and is now part of a team with Mike who has recently returned from Bird Island, to supervise the organization of the installations and the feeding of the animals. Teachers, retirees, shop workers, employees at the cannery and the administrative offices arrange to leave work as soon as they can and contribute to the rescue of the rockhoppers. Andy and I continue to work as a team and take on the delicate task of feeding the most vulnerable animals placed in quarantine in a space erected quickly behind the hangar. Throughout the day, we feed the birds a mixture of high-protein cat food and water, which we inject into their throats using a plastic tube connected to a syringe. Our lack of experience is sometimes disastrous, resulting in a misapplication of the tube that forces the penguin to regurgitate the nasty mixture right in our faces.

When the day is done, I go back to the house to take a shower before going out again to smoke a cigarette and take advantage of the stillness of the village, which the shipwreck had dispelled. I take the path that goes towards the port and stop on the promontory. Farther out, three imposing ships are anchored on a smooth sea and are bobbing slowly on the surface of the water. Among them, I recognize the *Austral*, forced to cancel its fishing expedition to lend a hand to the community.

'Don't think that it's always like this here!'

I'm startled, surprised by the voice, which is, however, familiar.

'You know, from the island's perspective, it's a true invasion. Since the fire at the cannery, three years ago, the place hasn't seen such activity.'

Meg comes up to the fence and looks out in the distance. It's been some time since I've seen her. I'm glad she's here.

'Mike saw the flames first. That night, he couldn't sleep. He went out to walk a bit, and that's when he saw the fire. The cannery wasn't at all like it is now. It was much smaller, less modern, too. Now, it is up to code, so there aren't any more of those problems of safety, hygiene and all those things you see on the mainland. It seems it's better like that.'

Meg puts her hand on my shoulder and looks at me, concerned.

'How are you, Ida?'

'I'm fine.'

9 April

Sometimes, Léon, it's like there are bumps, holes, sorts of mountains in my head. Strange noises, like thunder.

Everything is beautiful here. Everything. From the roiling surf to the smile of old Andy.

Ida

When I arrive, the bar is pretty much empty. A man, seated at the bar, is staring dully at the wall covered with pictures of houses from all over the world hanging over the rows of glasses and bottles of alcohol. Tom and Travis, caps on their heads, are sipping Castle Lites and talking. The two South

African logisticians I met the day before during a lunch break greet me warmly and order three more beers from Johanna, the owner of the Albatross Bar.

'We're glad to meet you. Travis and I worked for several years in Montreal, but, since we got back to the Cape, we rarely have the opportunity to speak French,' says Tom, taking a large gulp of beer. 'It's funny,' he continues, 'I have the impression I've known this island forever. I remember when I was a kid, I saw this little rock lost in the ocean on my map and I wondered who could live here, but I would never have thought I'd come here one day. It just goes to show, oil spills take you everywhere!'

A strong voice behind us cuts off the South African.

'It's rude to talk in French. Nobody can understand,' grumbles the man sitting at the bar.

Travis apologizes, visibly upset at having offended him.

The man with a military haircut leans on the bar and, out of despair or drunkenness, puts his head in his hands.

'Don't know the extent of the damage, but one thing's sure: it's not done. We're going to Bird Island soon to check on the rat traps set around the wreckage. If any vermin were on the boat, we're fucked; it takes only two to form a colony and fuck everything up. Because they're not content to eat garbage and such, they also eat albatross and petrel eggs— real carnage! Look, here, there's nothing left, you'd think you're on the moon!'

The forty-something man turns to the two logisticians:

'Do you want to come with us? It shouldn't take long, three, four days at the most, just enough time to empty the rat traps.'

'We'd love to, but we still have a lot to do,' Tom answers, obviously tempted by the offer.

'Can I come?'

The words fly out of my mouth even before I realize I've spoken them. The man looks at me, shocked.

'You want to go with us by yourself?'

'Yes,' I say.

The man smiles at me briefly, looks at his watch and leaves 2 pounds on the counter before walking out the door.

The two South Africans and I look at each other, mystified, then we take our glasses and go into the snooker room.

The ringing of the phone pulls me out of sleep and echoes in the room. Eight-thirty. Mike and Vera must already be at church. Who could be calling on Sunday morning at this hour?

'Hello?'

'Good morning, were you drunk yesterday at the bar?'

'Hello? Who's calling?'

'Sorry, it's Saul. We saw each other last night at the bar, with the two South Africans. Do you still want to go to Bird Island?'

'Yes,' I say, 'if it's possible.'

'OK, I have to get permission from the man in charge of the operation. But before that, I just wanted to be sure that you were thinking clearly yesterday.'

'Do you know when you're leaving?'

'The first day the weather is good.'

'That's perfect,' I say, seeing the sun flood into the room, 'the weather doesn't look too bad!'

'No, they've forecast a nor'wester. But don't worry, when I know, I'll call. I have to go. Bye.'

I hang up and go back to sleep until Vera, back from church, knocks on my door.

Please excuse me for taking so long to write you, Léon. The arrival of help has given us all a lot of work to do. Fanny is also on call for the penguins, and no longer comes to help Vera with the milking. So lately, I've been milking Suzy. In the beginning, it wasn't easy, but now, I think I'm doing pretty well.

I love you, Léon. So far away.

A few days later, Vera comes into the cabin where Andy and I continue to feed the penguins.

'Ida, Saul just called on the VHF, they're preparing to go to Bird Island. The boat will be setting off in an hour. Start getting your things ready, I'm stopping by the shop, then I'll come up to help you.'

I scarcely take the time to say goodbye to Andy, and run up to the house.

A few minutes later, Vera comes through the gate quickly, her arms loaded with two plastic bags filled with supplies. I blindly pack a few books, my sketchbook and some clothes. Mike parks his old pick-up in front of the house and loads three large water-proof bags on which my name is written.

At the port, the boat is ready to go. I just have time to slip on some water-proof pants and we're already setting off. The semi-rigid pulses and crashes against the waves, which are much higher at sea than in the enclosure of the port. In front of me, I recognize Saul, standing, framed by the pilot and two other men.

3

A thin layer of yellow lichen covers the sheet-metal walls of the old cabin. Saul takes a little key out of his pocket and opens the lock on the door.

The ray of light that travels through the room reveals a spartan and orderly interior: a stainless steel basin, a hot plate, three stools, a pile of magazines, a rickety cart over which hangs an array of rusty kitchen utensils. On the ground, large, damp, dark patches smudge the wooden planks that bend when you walk on them.

The smell of absence, of extended vacancy, exudes from the room; odours produced by a slow ripening of materials and objects left to themselves once the living have left and the door has been locked.

I've always thought that spaces have a hidden life, their own reality in which they unfold freely, not subjected to the world of humans and the contours of time. Sometimes, I imagine myself suddenly opening a door, unexpectedly climbing a hill and surprising the spectacle playing out before me.

Saul struggles with the creaking latches of the windows whose frames are covered with thick, badly applied layers of silicone. He walks into the adjoining room, picks up a thick, striped mattress that he places through the window and gives it several strong whacks.

'It's been quite a while since I've set foot in here. My father must have been the last one here. He's the one who built everything,' he says, looking around the space as if he were seeing it for the first time. 'We loved coming here when we were kids, it was a real change! OK, it's not Westminster, but you'll see, it's pretty nice.' His eyes complete their trip around the room and settle on me. 'I hope you're not afraid to stay alone at night, at least.'

How long has it been since I've slept in an empty house? Have I ever even done it? The question takes me back to old memories, memories I'd rather forget. In any case, Saul doesn't wait for an answer.

'Don't worry, there's nothing to fear here. You just have to be sure to shut the door well so the skuas don't get in—they'll eat your eyes, those rotten birds. The sea elephants will stay on the shore. No one has yet grafted legs onto them that I know of!' Saul gives a little laugh, but I'm not sure if he's joking or simply joyful. 'Come on, I'll show you the cabin where the guys and I are staying.'

Saul starts walking briskly on the narrow path that leads to the sea. Down below, there is a myriad of colourful huts, scattered on the edge of thick clumps of tussocks—those long grasses that carpet the hills—watching peacefully over the ocean. Stan's and Jimmy's voices escape from a minuscule green hut. The two guys are sitting on wooden planks located on either side of the door and sipping beers. When they see us, Stan opens two more and hands them to us.

'So, you see? You're going to spend the night in a true palace!' Jimmy says to me. His smile barely hides his shyness.

'Yes,' I say, 'but I don't feel right sleeping in a space that is ten times larger than yours.'

'No worries! You know, we've known each other since we were born. So, sleeping together isn't going to bother us!'

Stan starts talking. He talks fast. From what he's saying I can only follow the sounds that flow out and form a throbbing cadence in my ears. Outside the door, a few dozen metres away, a large swell rises and breaks on the shoreline, causing a huge explosion of spray to erupt with each new crash.

'*Bird Island, Bird Island for Meteor, do you copy? Over.*'

Stan puts down his beer and takes the walkie-talkie hanging on his belt.

'*Bird Island, go ahead.*'

'Hey, Stan, so now we're not worried. You've just arrived and already you're guzzling beer!'

A sharp burst of laughter comes through the speaker.

'OK,' the voice resumes, 'you're still fine with coming to lend a hand tomorrow on Long Island? Go ahead.'

Stan emits a burst of cursing, walks towards the crashing surf and points his finger at the icebreaker that is anchored not far offshore.

'Put down your binoculars, Pat, otherwise you'll be de-oiling the rocks by yourself! Go ahead.'

'Come on, we're counting on you. We'll meet you tomorrow at the Caves. It shouldn't be too rough. See you. Over.'

Stan is frowning. He puts the walkie back on his belt and joins us. I in turn leave the hut to get some air. Behind the row of little cabins, a steep slope rises up.

'Is it possible to walk up there?'

'Ah, these tourists, they're always in a hurry,' replies Stan with mock annoyance in his voice. 'Do you remember the seismologist who went back on the boat in October? Well, in two weeks, he swam in the Ponds, he came here, to Bird Island, he went to Stoney Beach, to the Caves, he climbed to the top and went fishing in Bath! Can you imagine?' Stan says to his two acolytes. 'In two weeks, he saw what most of us will never see before we meet our maker!'

Saul turns to me.

'Not to worry, we're not leaving right away. We'll have plenty of time to climb to the top. Now, it's time to get some food.'

In one movement, Jimmy and Stan finish their beers and get moving. The three men head towards a wide, rocky expanse located a few metres below.

'What's always hardest,' Saul says to me, his eyes scanning the rocks, 'is the first catch, because, before you can catch a fish, you first have to find some bait!'

He keeps searching intensely until his eyes settle on a rock over which a large swarm of flies is buzzing. He bends down and, with the tips of his fingers, picks up a rotting rockhopper.

Saul takes a knife out of his pocket, cuts the foot off the animal and puts it on a hook that he ties to the end of a line attached to a big, round reel. His movements are remarkably adept and agile. He hands the pole to me, smiling.

'Your turn to play, Ida!'

The reel sends the nylon line to the bottom of a narrow crevasse eaten into the rock by the sea. Soon, the other guys join me and throw out their lines. We don't say a thing, we're watching for the slightest tug of the nylon line that is shuddering between our thumbs and index fingers.

It's Jimmy's that tightens first. The slightly built man grabs the five finger that is jumping on the end of his hook, takes it off and cuts it into pieces so we can use it as bait.

In scarcely fifteen minutes, a dozen fish, whose distinctive sides are marked with five black stripes, are flapping on the warm, shiny surface of the rocky expanse.

Back at Saul's cabin, the only one with a hot plate and bottles of potable water, we get to work: we scale the fish, remove the filets and peel the potatoes that Saul takes one by one out of a huge canvas bag. Stan gets busy connecting a former car radio to a battery that he found at one of the radio-relay terminals.

During the meal, my plate resting on my lap, I watch the flame of the candle flickering under the vibrations of the pop music. Even if we don't talk a lot, the atmosphere is cheerful, almost joyful. Outside, the wind has chased away the clouds. The moon is so bright we can distinguish thin shadows falling from the tall grasses and tiny yellow birds pecking on the ground.

Bird Island

A quilt of colourful wool keeps me warm. On the nightstand, a candle stuck in the neck of a bottle, and, under my mattress, thousands of sharp little cries rise up from a carpet of birds.

Where am I?

Where am I, Léon?

I'm writing to you, incapable of telling you the date, an address, a point of reference. Since I arrived, I feel as if the world has stopped at the edge of my eyes, that nothing exists beyond the limits of my body, as if the entire world were enclosed in every detail, inside every little thing.

I light the candle and quickly put on my polar fleece and pants. In the next room, Saul, a headlamp around his forehead, is filling a dented kettle with water from a jerry can.

'Did you sleep well?'

'Yes, but it felt like I spent the night in a huge nest filled with birds. There's no chance I'll ever feel alone here!'

'It's because there's a gap between the floor and the rocks. At dark, the nightbirds hide under there.' Saul sets down the old kettle on the hot plate and strikes a match. 'We're going to help clean the oil on Long Island today, alright?'

I nod, smiling, and sit on one of the plastic crates we use as seats.

Saul takes two cups out of a cupboard he has trouble opening and tears open a small package wrapped in aluminium foil, out of which he takes two tea bags.

A few minutes later, Jimmy and Stan arrive, holding beers.

'We need to get going, mates. I've just received a call from Pat. They're putting the semi-rigid in the water, they shouldn't be long,' says Stan.

We swallow our tea, put on our boots, and set off. The wind has picked up during the night and causes the tussocks in front of us to wave around wildly. After walking for about fifteen minutes, we arrive at a cove teeming with sea elephants which the men chase away, gesturing and shouting loudly. Just then, the sound of a boat motor approaches. One of the two men on board throws out a rope that Stan catches and pulls slowly, so the pilot will have time to raise the motor to keep the propeller from getting tangled in the long, brown filaments that float on the water's surface. We get in quickly. The two men paddle, just long enough to get away from the seaweed, then we greet each other cheerfully.

'So, how's the camping?' one of the men asks me, laughing.

'Hey, since he's been staying on the icebreaker like a king, he thinks he's the big cheese, old Pat,' Saul replies, laughing.

'You're right, a boat like that costs a bundle! Anyway, the insurance companies have enough to pay for it. I'm not worried about them!'

The trip is short. In a few minutes, we land on a beach covered in algae and walk about a hundred metres before we come upon a horrifying scene: huge expanses of oil have painted the coastline black, and dozens of birds covered in oil are attempting in vain to pull themselves out of it. Crews are at work trying to keep the spill inside large floating devices made of white filaments that, connected together, form floating dams all around the zone.

The person in charge of the operation greets us and gives us what we'll need for the clean-up: jumpsuit, boots, gloves, mask, and earplugs. I'm on a crew with Jimmy. Saul and Stan, who are stronger, clean the rocks using a high-pressure hose. Jimmy and I spend the greater part of the day covering pools of water with microfibre cloths that absorb particles of oil before we start scrubbing the rocks using a small metal utensil the size of a teaspoon. The task is so enormous and the means for cleaning so paltry that, just as we start working, Jimmy begins to laugh hysterically.

'They must be crazy! We could stay here ten years,' he keeps repeating although his voice is lost in the deafening noise of the helicopter that, since the morning, keeps going back and forth between Long Island and the icebreaker.

Later, before it's completely dark, the semi-rigid comes to get us. Back in the cabin, Saul boils up the dozen lobster tails the boat pilot gave us. Jimmy opens a bottle of gin which we all gladly share.

That evening we laugh, actually, quite a lot. We laugh at the men's family stories, their childhood memories, we laugh about everything, nothing, at the pleasure of feeling joy light up our faces and of the sweet taste of gin spreading through our bodies and slowly making us drunk.

At some point, we wander over to the large, flat rocks near the coast. In the distance, the groaning of the sea elephants merges with the squeaking that comes out of the thickets. In front of us, the reflection of the *Meteor*, lighted by its two night lights, sparkles.

It's late now, I've had a lot to drink, and, before I allow sleep to overtake me completely, I get up and say goodnight to everyone. Saul insists on lighting the path for me, and walks me back.

At the cabin, he goes into my room and lights the candle.

'Do you know how to play matches?'

'No.'

Saul sits on the little bed opposite mine. The hundred metres we have just crossed have given me a second wind and, curiously, I'm no longer sleepy.

'I have seven matches between my fingers. We take turns choosing either one or two. You lose if you end up taking the last one.'

I take a match randomly. Saul takes two. We play for a long time, without stopping. As the time passes, I sense the darkness becoming heavy and weaving an opaque, reassuring covering around us. The game goes on until we become weary and our movements become mechanical, until the wax melts down and forms a long line that drips onto the blistered floor, until the candle is completely consumed and returns the darkness to the night. I can't see anything now. The dark has swallowed everything. I don't see a thing, but there are images. Slow, beautiful images that float and palpitate in the air, encouraged by a hand that, suddenly and unexpectedly, slowly begins to climb up the slope of my thigh.

That night, there are no landmarks, no coordinates to restrain us. All around, the ground liquefies, the walls melt one by one, they liberate a path that swallows up our desert mattress. Images, more images unfold, so many visions whose colours, smells and breaths carry me off, overwhelming me. And then there is that mass, that indescribable matter, that moving flesh in which I drown and which, both soft and powerful, buries me under its flank.

Bird Island.
This morning, I had to put my legs and my arms back in the right places. Put my head back on, too. The place where I was came back to me with the light. I could catch my breath, shake the sheets, make the bed, and cover it with the wool quilt. I'm warm. It's warm out. I don't know if it's the sun.

On the nightstand, a little piece of paper is lying next to a beer bottle dripping with cold wax and a box of matches.

We're on Long Island. I wanted to let you sleep. We'll be back soon. Take care.

Outside, a piercing light cuts through the shadows and thickens the landscape: ideal conditions for drawing. I take my things and sit on a rock that overlooks the long flat stones. Drawing empties me, absorbs me entirely. I need to feel completely accessible, because, even if experience has made the task less arduous, I must each time forget the way in which words fragment things and retain only the paths drawn by the light.

I want to capture everything, seize everything, allow every single thing to have a place in my sketchbook. Everything passes through it: the outhouse in the middle of the weeds, the string of multicoloured huts, the sea elephants piled up on the shore and, in the distance, the volcano that rises up, ever magisterial.

As the morning hours pass, the sun reaches its zenith and sucks up the shadows from the landscape which becomes dry and flat. I put down my pencil and sketchbook and decide to go fishing. The thought of surprising the guys with a warm meal when they return fills me with surprising joy.

I look around the flat rocks the way Saul did the day before, but it's no use. The rocks are deserted and the penguin whose foot he cut off has disappeared, as if our fishing party were only a mirage.

I go back to the cabin, hoping to find a piece of lobster from yesterday's meal. But, again, my hopes are short-lived; the men must have finished the fish this morning, because the pan is as empty as the flat expanse of rocks. I open the drawers of the little metal chest one by one looking for potential bait. Inside, rusty cans without labels sit next to packs of beer, and long expired bags of freeze-dried food, behind which I find a can of sardines.

The crevasse seems deeper than it did the day before, and the sea clearly more agitated. I bait my hook, taking care to do it just like the guys did, but the sardines are packed in oil, and are too slippery and flaky, they break apart one after the other just as I am putting them on the hook. After several vain attempts, I decide to wrap all the sardine filets around the hook using some thread. But once the line is in the water, the ball of fish falls apart and rises to the surface. Annoyed at my lack of *savoir faire*, I decide to bring in my line. At that moment, a huge mass jumps out of the water, and the gaping mouth of a shark in one gulp swallows the wad of sardines floating on the surface. Stunned, I manage to quickly reel in my line, scramble onto a rock and stay there, suspended on the side of the mountain, petrified. I gradually begin to doze.

When I wake up, the sun has begun to go down. I have a headache. In the distance, I hear what seems to be the sound of someone approaching before seeing a figure appear on the flat rocks while calling out my name in every direction. I call out in turn while waving my arms.

When he reaches me, Saul is dripping in sweat and can hardly catch his breath.

'We got back. You weren't in the cabin. I was afraid, Ida, really afraid.'

We both sit. Saul kisses me and lets his head drop down onto my legs.

It's night now and the soft dampness of the evening slowly moves in. Saul has fallen asleep. His head is heavy, but I feel good. He is handsome when he sleeps. He looks like a tortoise.

'Let's go back,' I whisper in his ear. 'We don't want Jimmy and Stan to worry. And imagine if they find us?'

Saul turns towards me. Two sapphire eyes pierce the night and look at me without blinking.

'I don't care, Ida. From now on, I don't care.'

It's only a cry, but it lasts all night long. A dull roar, continuous. And which releases, bursts forth, waltzes with wide steps. One night, just one night. The first and perhaps the only one. And so, even though the others might find us, even though the door might open, Saul doesn't care. Stricken with an impulse that urges him to flee, Saul breaks free, he runs as fast as possible, leaving behind forty years of drought, of close quarters, of 'you must,' of prayers and signs of the cross. To hell with morality, good behaviour and family drama. One night, just one night, the first and maybe the only one, drink in that skin, that island, that gift from heaven, that opportunity too unique not to seize it. Saul runs, abandoning one by one his roles as father, husband, fisherman, shepherd, a robust and responsible man, to offer me a naked body, stripped of conventions and standing, a dense, striking, almost unwieldy body, a collection of tight muscles, fashioned like a rock by the surf and the wind. And so, one night, just one night, detach one's hands from one's body and let them fly, explore the most unknown fields. Saul melts into me as I disappear into him, overwhelmed and inexpressibly happy to feel his body vibrate intensely as we live the impossible.

Bird Island.
My body chafed by the assaults of the sleepless night, I take my time forming my letters well. Saul. Who are you who

already knows me so well? And your precipitous body with an animal frame, your fossil body in which I burrow and which traverses the ages.

The same little torn bit of paper is on the nightstand. *We are on Long Island. I wanted to let you sleep. We'll be back soon.* The *Take care* was crossed out and replaced by *Miss you* written below. I kiss the paper and go off to draw.

Just as I do every time before I start drawing, I look through my sketchbook. It's strange, since I arrived here my drawings seem both emptier and denser, as if the purity of the landscape has blended into my stroke and rendered it more powerful. Something has left, has been released; my drawings are more porous, more permeable, they seem freed of a weight.

'Are we going fishing?' From below on the flat rocks, Saul is looking up at me, beaming. I run down the slope to join him.

'Jimmy and Stan are finishing up, helping the South Africans pack up the equipment on Long Island. The ice-breaker leaves tomorrow. I told them we'd take care of the meal.'

'The clean-up is already done?'

'No, work like that is never done, but at a certain point you have to pack it in.'

We walk towards the crevasse. A weak surf roils on the ocean's surface and fills the inside of the crevasse in waves. The image of the shark jumping out of the water is imprinted on the water's surface and reminds me of my failures of the day before, which, too ashamed, I decide not to mention. Saul prepares his line, unrolls it into the gap and stands motionless, entirely absorbed by the little jerks in the line between his fingers. I think he's handsome. His mouth, his eyes, he exudes something infinitely gracious. Suddenly, the line becomes taut. Caught off balance by the strength of the jerk, Saul almost falls backward. I rush towards him, put my arms around his waist and pull him backward with all my strength. We fall on the ground, but Saul gets up quickly so I can get up. Sitting on the rock, he looks for places where he can set his feet, but the stones are too smooth. A flood of curses flows out of his mouth.

'Go back behind me, Ida, you can help me.'

I do as he asks and sit down, my chest glued to his back. Together we pull, centimetre by centimetre, the dozen metres of line that separate us from the catch. Sitting between my legs, Saul uses his back muscles to reel the fish in. The line seems infinite to me, I struggle to follow its progress, because my feet are seized by cramps. As we continue to pull, we hear increasingly piercing cries.

'The hook must have caught a seal,' says Saul, his voice strained with his effort. 'It happens.'

At the end of interminable minutes of constant pulling, we discover a round, black shape hanging above the crevasse. A baby seal is struggling, rolled up in the line. Saul takes out his knife, slowly approaches the animal, and quickly cuts the nylon line, taking care not to get bitten. He then cuts a circle of skin around the hook and takes it out of the wound.

Paralysed with fear, the little sea elephant lies immobile where it lands.

Saul ignores it, and throws his line in the water again.

'Seal is the best bait you can find!' he says. But scarcely has he stopped talking when the line becomes taut again. This time, the strength of the catch is such that Saul is dragged off and becomes stuck behind a jutting rock that separates us from the crevasse. Saul rolls the line around his hand which, with the compression, becomes immediately red and swollen.

'I bet you it's a bloody fucking Cape mackerel,' Saul curses, without taking his eyes off the surface of the water, sliced by the line that is jerking under the frantic movement of a long form that we can see dancing and sparkling, lit by the rays of the sun.

I feel completely helpless, not knowing what to do to help him. I think of Hemingway, of that bitter struggle between the old man and the swordfish. I think of a child, of milky jellyfish. His arms bulging from the effort, Saul dances around the gap to find a better foothold and to keep the line from getting caught in the bushes growing along the sides.

Fighting for every millimetre, he gradually manages to raise the line, at the end of which a fish, with a magnificent yellow tail striking violently against the sides of the crevasse, is convulsing.

Saul makes a final effort. He yanks the line and falls backwards onto the ground. The Cape mackerel is enormous. Firm and hard like a tuna, it slowly dies on the flat stones. Without waiting to get up, Saul looks at me and opens his arms wide.

'We got him, Ida. We got him.'

The beating rhythm of the pop music and the steam coming out of the pots turns the room into an unexpected tropical dance hall.

The oil clean-up crews have completed their assignments and the *Meteor*, which has been anchored off the island for more than a week, is leaving to go back to the mainland.

Despite their fatigue, the guys laugh.

'You could spend your entire life scraping the rocks, but at some point you have to quit,' says Stan before pouring his beer down his throat without touching the bottle, as athletes do with their water bottles.

'In any case, they didn't scrimp on the equipment! We didn't even use everything,' Jimmy adds, his nose buried in an old fashion magazine in which three women in tweed suits pose with a dog.

'Yeah, I still say it's a good thing to do! Now, we can go on to more serious things,' says Stan, rubbing his hands together.

I look at him, questioning.

'No one's told ya? Tomorrow is the fat trip!'

'Didn't you come to check the rat traps?'

'Don't worry, that's for later. In any case, here everyone knows that it isn't some little traps that are going to stop the rats. Vermin like that can have ten litters before they get caught.'

'So what's the fat trip?'

'You'll see tomorrow,' Stan replies, looking complicitly at the others.

Bird Island.

I'd like to write with a single continuous stroke, without gaps or upstrokes. Just say, without telling. I'd like to find my tongue, let it beat its own rhythm. Because things have changed. Because the Earth has turned.

Saul sits down on the little bed opposite mine and turns the pages of a magazine faded by time. I pick up my sketchbook and lean back against the wall. Everything is calm, only the shadows of the furniture and objects dance in the candlelight.

'Have you told them?'

Saul takes my hand. His fingers are warm. I like when he caresses me.

'What happens on Bird Island stays on Bird Island. That's the rule, and everyone knows it.' His eyes are shiny. Two sparks. 'And, you see, I've taken off my wedding ring. Everyone knows what that means here.'

We look at each other for a long time.

'How do you begin when you draw a face?'

His question is endearing, childlike.

'I don't know, Saul. I've never asked myself the question. You begin with what you want. You know, eyes, a mouth, a nose, all that, they don't exist in drawing. We always think in terms of positive/negative, black/white, day/night, noise/silence. But in drawing, it's not like that. It's the light that guides you, it's what tells you what is somewhat light and what is somewhat dark, and it is out of those contrasts that shapes will emerge.'

Saul listens, attentive.

'Can you draw a radish for me?'

I burst out laughing. Saul looks at me, surprised.

'They say they're beautiful.'

Saul jumps onto the tiny bed and puts his head in the hollow of my stomach, right under my navel, as if he has found his spot. He stays there, for a long time, without moving, I continue to draw.

'I went to Europe once. My wife Bonnie was doing a training course on the Isle of Wight. When it was done, she insisted we go to London with the girls. I wasn't that keen on going. Cities, crowds, all that, never attracted me. On the street, I felt ridiculous, I thought everyone was looking at us. Bonnie told me I was imagining things, that we were like everyone else and there was no reason to feel ill-at-ease, but I know she wasn't comfortable, either. We took the Tube. It was the first time. People act as if it's no big deal, they consider it normal to travel underground, but it's bizarre, isn't it? At the hotel, there was a coffee machine. I think about it often. You put in a coin, push a button and a cup drops down. Hot coffee flows all by itself and stops right before the cup overflows. But the craziest thing was the minibar. In the room, behind the door, there was a fridge with dozens of little bottles of booze. I've never seen anything like it! We didn't stay in London long. A weekend, I think. The crosswalks, the little man who lights up and disappears to tell you when to cross, the noise, the people, all that, I'd had enough. Here, at least, we're lucky. And we have everything.' Saul stares at the ceiling, pensive. While he's talking, he lets his hand, criss-crossed with long purplish lines, travel between my side and my navel. 'Available women, that's the only thing lacking on the island. There's a choice between three or four. The fifth is either your sister or your cousin. I married my wife when she became pregnant. We hadn't really planned it. I was nineteen, she, eighteen. I had been drinking. I think she had been, too. It was at the end of an evening at the Albatross Bar. That's how Sarah was born. The rest, it's like with all the families. My father told me to go see Robby, Bonnie's father. That day he really gave it to me. It still hurts! The next day, he came to the house with a bottle. We fixed the date of the wedding, then we ordered materials to construct the house. You know, here, no one asks if he or she really loves his wife or husband. With Bonnie, we're different, but we try to make it work. In the summer, she loves to plan dinners at the house with the doctor and the administrator, but those dinners get on my nerves. I prefer the mountains or trips to the Caves. I really like going fishing with Mike, and sleeping in the cabin listening to the sea.'

Saul takes his eyes off the ceiling and raises his head, looks at me.

'Do you realize, on the island, I'm the only one who has ever been with a French woman.'

I smile, blow out the candle and let our bodies have their way.

I open my eyes. The world is blue from the two sapphires staring at me. Saul smiles and makes a tiny hole between his lips letting a little bit of air escape, whispering on my face. I feel his skin and, beneath his stomach, the yearning of his large penis. And I forget. I no longer dream. Why dream when this is reality?

Bird Island.
I'm on a desert island in the middle of the ocean. A man loves me. The cliché is such that I barely dare think it. And yet. I'm writing because it's true, because everything is true—the island, the man, the flat stones, the wind.

The dirt path beneath our feet goes along the coastline, overlooking a string of small coves invaded by series of huge waves intermittently breaking in generous clouds of spray. After we walk for a dozen minutes or so, the tiny path branches off and continues into thick clumps of tussocks that tower over us, masking the grey veil that is covering the sky. We walk in single file. Stan, leading, is whistling happily, digging up with a long wooden stick any plants blocking the path. Saul is at the rear. Without even seeing him, I sense the force of his gaze and the burn of his eyes on my back. Just as my mind is wandering, Stan stops.

'Here we are,' he says, setting down his stick.

We go into a large clearing surrounded by long, tall grasses and set down our things. The three men take a cloth bag, roll down their sleeves and quickly disappear into the tussocks, obviously in a hurry to get to work. Jimmy gestures to me to follow them, then slips between clumps of grass with the ease of a reptile. He stops opposite a hole the size of a big tennis ball and sticks his arm in up to his shoulder. He pulls it out suddenly, clutching a downy ball with light grey feathers in the middle of which emerge two small dark marbles and a black beak which the chick clacks frantically. Jimmy clutches the young petrel on either end of its neck, brings it down against his knee, and in a single movement bends his wrists to break the spine. The bird spits out a nauseating orange liquid and goes limp. Jimmy throws his prey into his sack and continues on his quest. I don't say a thing, I watch, horrified. After hunting for over an hour, and obviously satisfied with his booty, the slender man gives himself a little break, just enough time to rest a little and wipe off the tiny rivulets of sweat that course through the dirt covering his face.

'We're really lucky. Usually, at this time of year, the petrels have almost all gone. This year, they must have laid their eggs later. From what they say, the birds go as far as Greenland before coming back here in October, at the end of spring. But I tell you, it's better to come now to get the young ones, because a petrel with ten thousand kilometres under its wings is as hard as lead!' Jimmy talks without looking at me. I don't know if it's his shyness or because he is already looking for new holes. I'm glad he's talking to me.

Before going back into the clearing, I stay to watch Saul through the tussocks. He is sitting on the ground, in the middle of a large circle drawn by the tall grasses. I know he's looking for me, but I stay motionless in the thicket looking at that celestial body and the incredible presence, both robust and completely lunar, that emanates from it.

When I finally come out of the brush, his body gets up and starts walking to join me, but, probably recalling the presence of his two friends, he stops short and changes his mind, upset to be able to only look at me.

Above us, the dark veil that was covering the sky has completely dissolved and given way to a vast blue expanse untroubled by any cloud. It's warm, much warmer.

Sitting in the middle of the clearing, Jimmy and Stan, obviously satisfied with their catch, are stringing the petrels by their necks in order to carry the burden on their backs for the return hike.

When we get to the long, flat stones, the three men sit down in a line, their backs to the sea, and get to work.

One by one, Saul picks up a petrel from among the pile of feathers that the guys have poured onto the rocks. He inserts his knife in the neck and slices the animal to the rib cage. There, he raises the blade slightly and continues to descend to the tail before setting the bird down on his right side, in front of Jimmy who, with small, expertly executed cuts with his knife, takes off the skin. Stan, sitting at the far edge of the little processing factory, empties the petrels, scraping the inside bones with his fingers so as not to pierce the stomach. He then separates the fat from the birds' bodies, and slips the fat into a plastic bag so it can later be turned into oil. Motionless, I watch, fascinated by the speed and the ease with which the men work, their movements so synchronous that they look like they're emanating from the same body.

That evening, before nightfall, we go back to the cabin. Stan offers us a round of Castle Lite while Saul and Jimmy fill a large pot with bird fat which, when it's hot, emits clouds of tiny projectiles and fills the cabin with a strong odour of fried food. After drinking a few beers and uncorking a bottle of whiskey, the guys pour the fatty liquid and the non-dissolved bits into a large metal press that looks like a bellows and which, when squeezed, gurgles impressively.

For four days, we slice, sort, cut and salt the meat. The days go by and flow one after the other like pearls on a necklace. Working frees the mind and allows us to get to know each other without having to talk.

At the end of the first day, Stan suggests I take his place; he has to begin salting the meat and washing the containers in which it will be preserved. In the beginning, I'm hesitant and unsure of myself. The fat slides over my hands and makes the knife slippery, and several times I come close to slicing off my finger. But the guys, more amused than impatient, are indulgent and understanding. I learn quickly, and the next day they don't have to help me anymore. I work fast enough to follow their pace.

At dawn, the three men meet in front of the cabin before returning to the petrel nests and continuing their hunt. Later in the morning, I join them on the flat stones, carrying hot tea, beer and cold meat, which we eat together before resuming our places on the assembly line and preparing the birds to the beat of the music which drowns out the scraping of the knife blades and then is lost in the roar of the waves that crash against the shore.

The dancing light of the candle makes the shadows pulse and objects vibrate. Everything is calm. Outside, through the window, the volcano is slowly swallowed by the darkness. Saul is sitting in the adjoining room, one of the old magazines open on his lap. He's pretending to read to allow me to write, even though I know he wonders what purpose it might serve.

I blow out the candle. I like writing in the dark; some words are more modest than you might think and ask to be born in the darkness. I hear Saul get up and turn on the car radio. He asks if *like that* is too loud, or if *like that* is OK. When I light the wick again, the two pages of my notebook look like a musical score on which, half-way between writing and drawing, the symbols navigate between the lines. Saul enters the room softly. He takes off his watch, puts it on the nightstand, right next to his wedding ring, and lets his head settle into the hollow of my stomach, in the place which, from the first day, he has made his own. We remain silent for a long time, listening to the swelling cries of the nightbirds, until, emboldened by my caresses, the time comes for Saul to speak.

'I was in the dinghy that came to get you from the *Austral*. Mike was there, too. We all knew that you were going to stay at his house. While we were rowing out, before coming alongside, I told him he should go on board to greet you and introduce himself. That's how it's done. "Just do like they do in Europe," I told him. "People over there kiss each other on the cheeks to say hello." He thought I was teasing him and laughed. No surprise, in any case, he is much too shy! The bloke never raised his eyes throughout the loading and during the return trip he didn't move, his chin buried in the collar of his slicker. I saw you right away. You were wearing a red top with jeans and blue sneakers. You were holding onto the railing of the container, like that, with your fists closed. You seemed happy. Well, you were smiling. I wanted to say something to you, but I didn't know what. So I didn't say anything. It's stupid to be like that. But, you know, on the island we're not used to it. Well, maybe, the scientists, the doctor, the administrator and his family, the expats, right, but a girl alone, like you . . . That evening, in bed, when we were about to turn off the light, Bonnie asked me what was wrong. "You're different," she told me. The problem with Bonnie is that we know each other inside and out. I said no, I didn't see how I could be different, and I turned over to hide my smile. Your face, your smile, your way of looking at people. I remembered everything. So when I saw you at the Albatross Bar with the two South Africans, I didn't hesitate. Here, if you don't try once, you can wait your entire life! The two guys, I knew they wouldn't come—when you're on an assignment, you can't just take off. But I couldn't ask you directly. People would have found out. I was so happy, Ida, so happy when you asked if you could come! The day we left, I lied to Bonnie. I told her the two South Africans were coming with us. Otherwise, she would have found some way not to let you leave. Here, a woman alone with married men, it just isn't done.'

Saul's hand seeks mine, and squeezes it, not letting it go. Then he turns over and blows out the candle.

'Ida, Ida, Ida, Ida fire, Ida laugh, Ida blue, Ida fly, Ida life. Ida.'

A celestial voice chants my name in my ear. I close my eyes and fall asleep. At peace.

Every morning with a leap
The sun takes root on my face.
I seize that burning light like a rudder.

The poem comes back to me, emerging from the depths with the first light of day bouncing off my skin and pulling me from sleep.

Saul is sitting on the little bed across from ours, a steaming mug of tea resting on the mattress. Through the window he watches Jimmy and Stan walk away, carrying a pack of beer and a bag.

'They're going to check the rat traps near the wreck, on the west side of the island, before we pack up and head back.'

Saul turns his head and looks at me.

'Sleep well?'

Head back. The words fall like blows of an axe. Head back. And here I had thought that the island was immutable, that time had stopped. Head back. But to go where, go back to whom?

Saul puts his mug on the nightstand, kneels next to me and puts his forehead on mine.

'The oil clean-up, the petrels, the rat traps—we've done what we came to do, now it's time to go, the mission is complete. It's time to go, Ida. And you know, we don't have a lot of drinking water left and there's no fresh water on the island.'

Saul holds my head between his hands and kisses me, covering my tears of anger with his kisses. Playful, tricky, the island has gotten the better of me; it has burst the glass bubble that protected us, dissolved the beneficent boundaries that made our isolated community the centre of the world. Head back. How could I have been so naive? How could my mind have shut down like this?

'It's gonna be fine, my dear. It's gonna be fine. I'll make a plan, Ida. Nobody can separate us. Do you hear me? Nobody.'

I look up. Around me, I see the cans of deodorant, the beer bottles piled on the shelves, the burnt-down candles, the wool quilts, the old, dented kettle, the disorder, the arrangement of the furniture, the crates, the things. I smell the hot odour of grime. It's strange how it all seems familiar to me; I feel as if I've always lived here, and worse, that I've never lived at all before this.

Saul hands me the tea and plugs the speakers into the transponder battery. Some lively music echoes in the room. Track 3, his favourite. He picks up a candle and turns it into a microphone, and, standing on the bed, begins to sing, making me laugh:

Deep in the night
I'm looking for some fun
Deep in the night
I'm looking for some love
De-de-de-deep in the night
I'm looking for some fun
Deep in the night
I'm looking for some . . .

Saul. Your eyes are sparkling. Saul, inimitable Saul. I look at you, I observe you, seizing this moment the way one gathers wood in autumn in preparation for a cold winter.

When Jimmy and Stan join us on the flat rocks, we finish gathering up the driftwood that we gathered—not without some trouble—throughout the afternoon, because, that morning, Saul had the idea of having a braai—a traditional holiday barbecue—before our departure.

Stan makes a little circle with some stones behind a rock that protects us from the wind. In it he places some of the driftwood and a bit of crumpled paper. Large golden flames quickly surge up from the little pile of wood and paper.

The night has fallen. Bits of fat drip from the skewers of petrels, making the embers crackle. Saul opens a pack of beer and a bottle of brandy which he passes around. Stan turns on the radio. The music sounds over the rocks.

> *I had no illusions*
> *That I'd ever find a glimpse*
> *Of summer's heat waves in your eyes*
> *You did what you did to me,*
> *Now it's history, I see*

No one knows the words, but everyone sings.

> *Here's my comeback on the road again*
> *Things will happen while they can*

Stan goes to the shoreline and begins to dance barefoot on the flat stones, a bird kabab in one hand and a beer in the other. All three of us join him, carried away by the drunkenness of this dark night.

I will wait here for my man tonight
It's easy when you're big in Japan

Jimmy is completely drunk.

Biiiiiiig in Japaaaaaaan.

He's shouting; his cries travel away and are lost in the ocean. This evening, we laugh a lot, with simple and unadulterated joy.

It's already very late when, depleted of breath and energy, I lie down next to the fire, hugging in my arms a long, roundish stone. Before sleep completely overtakes me, I feel someone shaking my shoulder. I open my eyes. Saul holds out his hand and helps me stand up.

'You can't stay here, Ida. It's too dangerous. There could be skuas. Those beasts are real demons, they even eat their own young. At night, they fly in the sky and form a large circle around their prey before diving all together onto their victim—they go for the eyes and pull them out with their beaks. That's how my dog lost his sight.'

Stan clears his throat and pushes the button on the walkie.

'*Island radio, Island radio for Bird Island, do you copy? Over.*'

Sitting, pressed together in Stan and Jimmy's cabin, we are hanging over the crackling of the speaker out of which there is no response. Stan repeats his request and hardens his voice to give it more volume.

'*Island radio, Island radio for Bird Island, do you copy? Over.*'

After several attempts, a voice finally crackles out of the radio.

'Stan, my man, how's it going? We thought you were dead!'

A loud laugh overwhelms the sound of the radio. Stan, obviously relieved to have established a connection, holds the radio out and lowers the volume.

'Hey, you're not in a hurry, eh, Pat! Yeah, it's OK, and no, we're not dead yet. OK, in case you're interested, we've checked on the rat traps. All empty. So, from that side, nothing to report. We've also caught all the birds; we have enough to last quite a while! So we're ready, now, whenever you want! *Go ahead.*'

'Ok buddy! But it ain't possible now, there's bloody north-east winds, I'm telling you, you'd think it was July! There hasn't been a fishing day since you left. OK, call me back tomorrow around 7 a.m., before work. I'll check the weather with the guys, because I don't know how this is going to shape up. *Go ahead.*'

'Ok buddy, tomorrow at 7. *Over.*'

'Talk tomorrow. *Over.*'

Stan pushes the little black button on top of the radio and turns towards us.

'Ok, now, we just have to wait, guys.'

Saul and I walk back on the path up to the cabin.

'So here we go again!' he says to me, not holding back the smile that covers his face.

'Yes,' I say, 'we have a little reprieve.'

I'm happy he shares my happiness. All night long, I had secretly hoped to be able to eke out another day and soak up his presence for a little while more.

We have just come into the cabin when we hear a loud knocking on the front door. Stan opens it and bursts into the room.

'I can't believe it! That fat tub 'o lard Pat didn't give me the right key.' Stan sits down and continues, not catching his breath: 'Earlier, right after the call, I saw that the talkie's battery was really low, so I went to Pat's hut to look for the charger. But of course he gave me the wrong one, it must be his garage key he gave me because it doesn't open a damn thing!'

'The battery's almost dead?' asks Saul.

'Yeah, see for yourself!'

Still angry, Stan takes the radio off his belt and hands it to Saul who turns it on. There is only one bar out of the five needed for a fully-charged battery.

'OK,' says Saul, with a serious voice, 'we'll have to use it sparingly.'

At dusk, Saul suggests we take a walk to West Point. After spending three months underground, the petrels use the cover of dusk to leave their dens and take flight.

We walk hand in hand on the path that glows with the last amber rays of the setting sun. A light, cool wind moves the tall grass that continues as far as the eye can see. We arrive close to a long, sloping rock that bars the path, and Saul tells me to sit down. In front of us, a huge colony of white and brown birds are dancing and spinning above the sea. Their sharp little cries join the long groaning of the sea elephants that press together on the shore and pile up on top of each other.

Saul taps me on the shoulder and points in the direction of the rock. Some young petrels with milky plumage are gradually coming out of their burrows and jumping around, some behind others, patiently waiting their turn to get to the rock. Once they reach the end of it, they throw their little bodies into the void and suddenly unfold their immaculate wings to join the imposing carpet of birds that is waving in the sky.

Gripped by the beauty of the spectacle, I let my gaze waltz between the sky and the earth. In front of me, Saul's profile waves above the horizon, bathed in the last rays of the sun.

Bird Island, last night.
His head fits onto my stomach, like a missing puzzle piece.
　　What can I say? What can I write? I feel good. I expect nothing. The wind is blowing outside. Keep blowing.

Armed with his headlamp, Saul quickly goes down the path. I try to follow him, doing all I can not to slip on the stones; it had rained during the night and the path is a water slide. Saul hurries. We're late. Late. Saying that word, I realize just how foreign that feeling had become.

Stan and Jimmy, huddled on the wooden planks that serve as their beds, are waiting stoically. When they see us, Stan, who takes his role as walkie-operator very seriously, turns it on.

'*Island radio, Island radio for Bird Island, do you copy? Over.*'

In the absence of a response and aware of the risk involved in not having a battery, Stan begins to get angry.

'Fuck Pat. I'm guessing he's in the fucking sack and hasn't turned on his bloody radio.'

No one speaks. We just hear Jimmy's shivering and his teeth chattering. His sleeping bag is soaked. There must have been a leak in the roof and the rain must have come into the hut during the night.

Despite his exasperation, Stan continues.

'*Island radio, Island radio, Island radio for Bird Island, Bird Island, do you copy? Over.*'

After waiting several long minutes, a voice finally interrupts the crackling of the walkie.

'*Tristan, go ahead, Stan.*'

'What the fuck are you doing, Pat, are you still in bed, or what?'

'Stop being an arsehole! Today isn't a good day, guys. Too much swell in the port. You'll have to call again tomorrow.'

'Hey, listen Pat, you really fucked up with the key. Is it your garage key you gave me, or what? Because now, we're running out of battery for the walkie. We're really fucked.'

'Shit!' Pat cries. 'I screwed up! OK, I won't stay on. Good luck, guys. I'll talk to you tomorrow, same time. Over.'

Stan doesn't bother responding. He turns off the radio and sits opposite Jimmy whose face is ashen.

'We'll be OK, mate, we'll be OK,' he says, tapping him on the back, but his heart isn't in it.

After we insist that Jimmy join us, we all wander back to Saul's cabin, which is more comfortable and sheltered from the wind, but the atmosphere is gloomy, no one speaks; Pat's call has really disturbed us.

Even before finishing his tea, Jimmy returns to his bunk in the hut. Stan, Saul, and I start looking for a first-aid kit for Jimmy and some disinfectant for Stan who cut his finger when he was picking up the rat traps; the wound looks bad and is beginning to get infected. For two hours we open old trunks of clothes, look through piles of magazines and the grimy bottoms of cupboards. In vain, no first-aid kit.

'It must be in Pat's treasure chest along with the walkie charger,' grumbles Stan, who hasn't lost his sense of humour.

Saul is taking advantage of the search to do a bit of organizing and takes some cans out of drawers 'in case we have to stay longer.' He also throws out the Cape mackerel that he found covered in maggots in spite of the rag he had wrapped it in. Mainly, we're beginning to run out of fresh water. So Saul asks me not to wash anymore. 'Or maybe just a little, because you're a woman.'

Bird Island, last night.
My hand, folded in front of my eyes, forms a little peephole in which his image appears. I let his body move through my

clasped fingers. His body. That vast menhir, that vaporous anchor.

Not knowing where to look, Saul smiles, ill at ease, then he starts playing my game, takes my imaginary camera and turns it onto him, as if he's filming himself. 'I love you, Ida,' he murmurs before returning it to me.

His head resting on my stomach, Saul watches the cloud of flies that hover around the room.

'I don't know who's taking care of them.'

'What?' I ask.

'Sorry, Ida, I was thinking out loud. I don't know who is taking care of the cows while I'm gone. Usually, on Saturday, I'm the one who moves them to a different pasture. I was wondering who's filling in for me.'

Saul is silent for a moment, still watching the flies buzz around the room.

'You know, on the island, we live on a tiny little stretch of land stuck between the sea and the volcano. There isn't much space for the animals, and the grass grows very slowly because of the wind. And so, we have to move the herd regularly and be careful there aren't too many animals in one spot. Each family has two cows and each person has a sheep. There's no choice. It's the same rule for everyone.'

'What do you do when someone new moves in? Do you give them a cow and a sheep?'

Saul looks at me and smiles, obviously amused by my question.

'No! Outsiders aren't allowed to settle down on the island. The arrival of a new family would increase the number of inhabitants and thus of cows needing to graze, which means there would be even less space available. The only way someone can settle there is to marry someone from the island.'

Saul looks at me and smiles.

'Are you interested?'

I laugh so I won't have to answer him, and let my hands slide down his face slowly.

'On the island, no one has ever divorced yet,' Saul says, his eyes closed.

It has become a ritual. Every morning we make the same pilgrimage and, every morning, the words are the same: 'Too bubbly in the harbour and bloody shitting northeast wind.'

Stan curses, Jimmy shivers, Saul is silent. The more days that go by, the longer time seems. Between two radio calls, we spend twenty-four hours in suspense, without knowing if we'll have to pack our bags or figure out what to eat the following day. Jimmy is having trouble eating and stays in the hut lying down. Several times a day I bring him a bit of warm tea and petrel drumsticks. Sometimes I stay with him, I wait for him to eat, and I bring back the dish.

That afternoon, I paint birds on the wall. Saul asked me to do it.

'That way, you'll be here every time I come back.'

While I paint on the cabin walls, Saul opens the cans that he takes one by one out of the drawers. Most of the contents must be rotten because he swears each time he opens a new one. Seeing that the canned food won't be enough, he takes some little silver containers out of a drawer.

'A few years ago, some Russian soldiers held manoeuvres here. When they left, we found entire cases of survival rations. I kept some. So that . . . well, one can never be too careful . . . ' he says, placing the cans on the sink.

Bird Island, last night.
Last night, I dreamt of skuas. They came in through the window and tore out our viscera through our ears. When I woke up, Saul's eyes were wide open. Saul is a beacon—he watches more than he sleeps, always on guard, never at ease. 'You're not sleeping?' I asked him. Saul turned and looked at me. For a long time. 'It was good,' he told me. His eyes were shining.

Like every morning for the past four days, the departure is put off until the following day, and, like every morning for the past four days, Pat assures us he will come get us . . . if the sea is OK, if the wind changes, if the weather allows. With each new call, our departure seems ever-more hypothetical and distant, like a meeting that is so postponed that it becomes unnecessary.

We pretend to keep busy, aware that our activity is only a pretext to make the day shorter. Everyone assigns themselves tasks to accomplish, goals to achieve, to fill the time until the next call. This morning, Saul gets it in his head to organize the storeroom of the cabin. Stan empties a drawer filled with cutlery outside in front of the cabin, and sharpens the knives one by one on the edge of a stone. Jimmy is paler and paler. For three days, he hasn't left his bunk and lies prostrate in the hut which is horribly cold and damp. I sit on a rock looking at the volcano which has never seemed so far away.

After the storeroom has been organized, Saul suggests we walk up to the top of the mountain.

'It's the first thing you wanted to do when we arrived. Remember?'

Yes, that's true. I had completely forgotten, as that day seems to go back years now.

Saul hands me a stick. We take the path and head left through the tussocks. We climb slowly, helping each other, like two old people. The slope is steep, but the mountain isn't tall, and, in less than an hour, we reach the top—a little bald dome encircled by tree ferns.

I look up. Huge, and stretching out in all directions, the sea is there, watching us. Huge, gigantic, its blue surface blending with the sky and forming a smooth and homogeneous sphere around us.

Behind me, Saul is observing. We are facing the same landscape, and yet I know that we're not seeing the same thing. And that fascinates me. I am enthralled by his ability to decipher signs in nature, to interpret the rustling of a leaf, the stance of a bird or the rippling of water. At his side, I feel deaf and blind, incapable of establishing the slightest link between what I see and what it indicates to me.

Saul places his head in the hollow of my shoulder and encircles my torso with his two, muscular arms.

'Before, in the summer, in January, we came here in a long-boat for holidays. The trip took almost the entire day. I really loved it. They were beautiful boats, and sturdy, too, they were more than 30 feet long. We arrived over here and landed there,' he says, cutting the air with his finger, 'even if, some-times, the wind was spinning so fast that, in mid-journey, we were forced to go back and return to port. "Only the unex-pected is certain," that's what the old-timers here say. Each longboat had its own crew. With Mike and the guys, it took us more than three years to build ours. I'm telling you, that's nothing next to what my father and his brothers did. In those days, they covered the hull with canvas and animal skins—there was no resin or fibreglass. But, now, all that is over. Longboats are sitting idle in front of the administrator's house. They require more maintenance than semi-rigids, so they aren't used anymore.'

Saul suspends the slow flow of his words, then resumes:

'It's a pity. There is nothing more beautiful than the sound of the wind in the sails.'

We stay for several hours, our gaze sucked in by the blue of the landscape. Before the sun reaches the horizon, Saul comes close to my ear.

'Shall we run?'

Without giving me time to answer, he grabs my hand and takes off through the tussocks. Drawn by the void, we speed down the slope. Our feet fly off the ground and race through the tall grass. And we shout out, we howl like mad dogs, like two wild children, like two lovers crazed to feel the air strike their faces, the hand of the one grasping that of the other.

This day is the last, like every day for the past five days, a thousand years, three centuries. Henceforth, it's all the same.

After the call this morning, Saul goes back to bed. His throat is covered with white spots. He whistles when he breathes. I'd like to be able to help him, make him some tea, but there is now only some twenty centimetres of water left in the jerry can.

While waiting for the time to pass, I draw; the cloud of microscopic flies that you swallow when you breathe, the candle stuck in the neck of a sherry bottle, the wind that blows, the shutters that bang, Saul's dirty, arched feet that hang over the bed, all those things have been drawn so much that I feel I've exhausted them. Lying next to me, Saul wakes up from time to time. I've stuck two cushions behind his back to help him breathe, but he's coughing more and more.

Last night, when we got back from the mountain, we finished the survival rations. And so, this afternoon, I look in the cupboard for something to eat. I find some flour that I mix with some petrel fat and fry the mixture up. The guys seem to like it. Even Jimmy eats what I bring him.

Bird Island, last day.
I've never believed in God. I've never prayed. But, for the first time, I'm addressing You.

You, the wind, the swell, the currents. You, the sun and the moon. We came, we stayed, so now, help us get home.

The departure is again postponed. Saul goes back to bed, without sleeping, like yesterday. I'm cold, I'm hungry, I'm afraid. Or maybe not, or maybe nothing. I don't know. I don't know anything. I write. The only string I still manage to hold onto to connect my words and maintain a bit of reality.

It's unbearable to feel yourself at a stand-off every day. Like on a mat. Like in a prison. Detained or freed. Freed or detained. An island-prison, like in novels. I hate novels.

And the white spots on Saul's throat. And Jimmy's shivering. Fucking rat traps, fucking sea, fucking island. I hate islands.

The wait. Again the wait, the one that forces us to confuse the moment with duration and duration with eternity.

Calm down, Ida.

Saul whistles more and more when he breathes. I'm afraid, I'm cold, I'm hungry. I don't know anything, but help, please help, give us your hand.

Bird Island.
I can't think anymore. Survival erases any abstraction. I can't reflect: I do. What a body can do. Writing is the only thing that still seems possible, but without my head or my brain. My hands will decide, they know. I tell them: 'Like in the dark, do like in the dark.' They know.

Seven a.m., like every morning, we join Jimmy and Stan in their hut. Outside, it's pouring rain.

'The weather window is extremely narrow. We get underway in twenty minutes. Meet at West Point. You have to be ready. Over.'

Pat's words are dry and choppy, he talks like a robot. It's not the time to applaud, not the time to rejoice. We go back to the cabin and begin getting our things together. Backpacks, empty jerry cans, garbage bags, gas canisters, buckets of petrels.

We go back and forth between West Point and the cabin. I have trouble walking straight and keeping my balance; the buckets of meat are terribly heavy and the path that leads to the cove in the pouring rain is as slippery as an ice-skating rink. The cove of West Point is invaded by skuas and sea elephants that Saul and Stan attempt to chase away by waving their arms and shouting. Jimmy is sitting on a rock. His head and his hands are buried in his raincoat. He looks like a big yellow bag.

Everything happens very quickly: once the dinghy is anchored, we form a chain from the cove to the boat to load our things. The water comes up to my hips when two men in raincoats hold out their arms to drag me on board. The guys get in and the dinghy sets off.

At sea, a strong swell turns the boat, and it rises with each wave. I clutch the side and don't let go. The men, happy to see each other, shout over the roar of the motor. In the middle of the group, Saul, like a statue, stares into the distance.

4

The water that streams out of the showerhead runs down my back and slowly dissolves the shell of grease, dirt and sweat that was encasing my body. I stand there, not moving, watching the dozens of little blackish rivulets running down my thighs and spreading slowly in the water on the shower floor before running down the drain. And I cry because I am unable to hold it in, realizing, at that moment, the unbridgeable distance that now separates me from Saul and Bird Island.

1st Day

Here I am, stuck. Vapid, useless. A plant without roots. No more birds under my mattress, no more fluttering of wings, indistinct rustling. And the odour of life that covered your skin? The urgency of your breath, the bitterness of the whiskey. My eyes are empty, my body is empty, lost in this gigantic bed, in this heap of foam that is much too soft and comfortable for me.

How can I begin again? How can I land? Find joy again.

For three days we've been glaring at each other without really knowing what to say or how to talk to each other. The island and I. Alone among the furniture and household things, I spend my days with my nose glued to the window looking out at the sea, intermittently wiping away the patch of mist that fogs the horizon. Sometimes a fly lands on the window and moves around my hand. It's odd, but its legs leave no trace on the condensation, I wonder how it stays on. Then the fly flies away and lands on a doily on which a wooden frame with the photo of a dog has been placed. And my hand slides over the condensation, wiping a long path that gradually allows me to see the wall of lava stones that encircles the green grass of the yard.

Then Vera arrives, always at the same time. The gate bangs shut and the two dogs start barking. I hurry back to the desk that Mike had set up in the middle of the sitting room. I remove the cap from a pen, open a book at a random page and pretend to work to hide my distress.

I would like her to come into the room, talk to me, smile at me, ask me how I'm doing. But Vera only glances at me and disappears into the garden, returning a few minutes later carrying a laundry basket. Then I sit on the sofa and stay there, watching her.

It's strange, since my return, I feel as if my body is escaping me, as if it is being drawn by the slightest human presence, like new-borns who, when they wake up, search the space, seeking warmth and skin and the assurance of a voice. I need flesh. I need sounds, even small ones, even porous ones, to rekindle the breath that is still vibrating in me and to control the loss that is consuming me.

Across from me, Vera sets up the ironing board and starts ironing the clothes, her movements relaxed. Her blond ponytail waves in the air as she navigates the iron in between the folds of the clothing. A true grace emanates from her movements, a great femininity. She looks like a goddess, a saint, a secret being who has escaped from a fable.

Then, suddenly, the young woman raises her head, as if she has just noticed my presence.

'Having a nice day?'

'Yes, a nice day.'

Then, nothing else; only the steam from the iron and the rustling of the ironed sheets.

The afternoon is winding down when suddenly a long series of vibrating sounds arise from the village and reverberate in the room.

Sitting at the kitchen table, Vera immediately stops peeling potatoes, gets up and washes her hands.

'The mail is here!' she says, almost joyfully. 'It's Bonnie, my sister-in-law. After the boat is unloaded, she rings the gong to let everyone know that the mail is being handed out. You know, the empty red propane can hanging behind the hall?'

What she says has the effect of a bomb exploding in my face.

'Bonnie, Saul's wife?'

'Yes, that's right.'

'You mean Saul is your brother?'

'There are four of us in the family. Saul is the oldest. By the way, he isn't very well right now. Yesterday, after the unloading, Mike and I went to see him; he hasn't gotten out of bed since your return from the island. The doctor is keeping him home for two weeks and . . . '

Vera keeps talking, but I don't hear her anymore.

Her fair complexion, the clarity of her gaze, the fine lines around her eyes. How could I have missed the resemblance, hidden the evidence so blindly?

So I was going to meet Bonnie. Thinking as far back as I can remember, at no time did Saul describe his wife to me; and I, myself, had never imagined her. And yet, it's a fact: the wives of men do exist.

The municipal hall is a large, white cinderblock building located in the middle of the village. Inside, close to a hundred women and old people are sitting on benches, their backs leaning against the walls; children are running around, taking full advantage of the emptiness of the space. I sit down next to Vera, on one of the rare, still-vacant spots. At the other end of the hall, three women are emptying large canvas sacks filled with dozens of letters and packages onto a wide wooden counter. No one is speaking, only the sounds of crying babies and the noise of packages banging when they fall out can be heard.

Then one of the women takes a letter from the top of the pile and, with the assurance and solemnness of a professor announcing a prize, proudly states the name of the recipient.

I'm guessing she's Bonnie; her proud carriage, her expansive movements. A great determination emanates from the woman, an undeniable good nature which, however, doesn't completely mask a certain pleasure in holding the privilege of passing out the mail and, from that fact, enjoying true power within the community.

I watch her as she announces one by one the names of the lucky recipients who, triumphant, get up one after the other to get their mail.

Does she know? What does she know? How can the wife of a man not be aware of such things?

The hand that taps my arm makes me jump.

'Ida, Bonnie's calling your name, you have mail,' Vera whispers in my ear.

I quickly stand up and discover hundreds of eyes riveted on me. I go up to the counter. The plump little woman greets me with a wide and frank smile.

'This is for you. Probably news from France!' Bonnie says, holding out a letter without letting it go, as if she wants to force me to raise my eyes so she can better drive hers into mine.

4th day.
I'd like to be irreproachable, have nothing to confess. And yet, I don't regret a thing. The words, the taste, the movements. Nothing.

For five days I've been walking on the same road that leads from the lava field to the potato fields and from the potato fields to the lava field. I walk, pushed by the wind that whirls between the hills, with the sea and my stick as my only companions.

Walk, advance, find a mechanical rhythm to distance my thoughts from myself; reach the huge pile of golden-tan sand that obstructs the road and turn back. Continue, go by Runaway Beach, Hillpiece, Big Sandy Gulch, go across Hottentot Gulch, climb over the metal bars that keep the cows off the road, go into the village, keep going to Little Green Hill. It looks like Scotland, with stone walls, no less. Maybe Ireland.

Occasionally, huge rocks break free from the cliffs and roll along the slopes, up to the edges of the houses, causing a deafening din. Then nothing; the sound of the sea and the blowing of the wind.

One day, two days, three days, four days, counting my steps, striding along, looking at the summit of the hills and starting again, always starting again, guided by the road like a tight-rope walker on her wire.

Then one day I crack. I grab the handle of the gate, go inside, open the fridge, take out the jug filled with the milk from Suzy, the cow that I help Vera milk every morning, take the little concrete path that leads me to the Albatross Bar, and continue to the end of the path. I know where he lives. Saul told me one night, on Bird Island.

His house is similar to all the other houses on the island: a front door made of dark wood, a square of grass surrounded by a wall of lava stones, a red sheet-metal roof. Windows, too, with vinyl frames. Just as I put my hand on the gate, a teenaged girl comes out of the house, alerted by the barking of the dog. I suddenly want to disappear, to run away; I had never, at any moment, imagined that at this hour of the day Saul wouldn't be alone. But the girl is only a few metres away. In one movement, she calms the border collie, opens the gate and gives me a shy smile. I mutter a few words in pitiful English and hold out the pitcher of milk to her, doing my best to stop trembling and not drop the milk. The girl takes it and disappears into the entryway, politely pretending not to notice my distress.

'Dad, it's the French lady,' she announces laconically while passing through the door.

A raspy voice invites me to an adjoining room. Saul is lying on a green sofa, across from a huge TV screen showing two GIs running after vampires, armed with massive flame-throwers shooting out impressive blue flashes. He turns around slowly, like an old man, and invites me to sit down on a little blue stool. To avoid an awkward silence settling in, he launches into some small talk: the cow he killed Saturday for his father-in-law; the work he won't return to until the following week; the pills the doctor gave him which give him a headache; the fishing season that will soon be getting under way.

I look at him, watching for the tiniest sign, the slightest call, the faintest inflection of his voice. But nothing; no word stands out, nothing he says leaks anything, his broken voice offers me only smooth, controlled, horribly barren words as the only elixir.

'How are you?' he asks me suddenly.

'Me?'

I'm incapable of speaking, of putting together a sentence. His daughter is there, right in the next room, and soon his wife and his other daughter will arrive to feed the dogs and prepare dinner. So I swallow, I gulp down one by one the words that were pounding in my head during the days of empty walking, without taking my eyes off the tight little links in the carpet underneath my feet. His daughter delivers me from my silence by coming into the room carrying a tray containing a plastic sugar bowl and two teacups out of which a thin stream of steam is drifting up, free, voluptuous. Steam is beautiful. Then I abruptly stand up and apologize for coming, for being one too many, I think to myself. I hold my hand out to the man, to this new stranger, slipping a tiny piece of paper into his as we shake.

And I walk. Keep walking. The fields, the road, the dull sound of the silence and the whisper of wind that knocks against my head. It's cold. I'm suddenly very cold. My head is full of aching.

8th day.

For two days, the question haunts me and tortures my mind: Is clandestine love necessarily false?

And I keep walking; even at night, I walk. At night, I walk in the ditches. I'm at the same level as the road, my face opposite the asphalt. No one sees me. Not the rare cars that go by, not the dogs, not the cows. I walk exposed in the ditches, my head lowered so I won't be seen. No one must see me.

When night falls, I climb Hillpiece to watch the dozens of little windows of the houses gradually break free from the darkness and form a vast constellation. When I sit down, I notice a slight rustling in the pocket of my jacket; I take out the letter that Bonnie had handed me a few days earlier. Thin and curvy, I recognize Léon's handwriting.

Léon.

A very small piece of wilted paper is floating inside the envelope.

Ida, my Ida,
How can I wait when, at long last, the promise of seeing you is finally here.
    A place on the next boat.
    I'm coming.
    L.

A light breeze has picked up, slowly moving the grass on the hills that border the shore. In front of me, the little village is sleeping, buried by the night.

That night, I am unable to sleep. You've invited yourself, indelible, under my closed eyelids.

How could I have forgotten you, Léon? Have I really forgotten you?

But it's no use: I turn the image over and over again in my head; unthinkable, impossible to imagine you here, walking on this land, among these people.

The next day, very early, I run to the Internet cafe and let the words slide out of the black keyboard.

There are spaces where everything vacillates. Where every-thing leaves. Certainties, desires, the thirsts of before.

Everything is expanding, Léon, dissolving absolutely.

I no longer know who you are. I no longer know who Léon is. I no longer know if Léon exists.

So I'm telling you, I'm begging you: don't come, Léon.

I would be unable to welcome you, be close to you, talk to you.

Goodbye, Great Eagle.

Goodbye.

Ida

Coming out of the little white building, I suddenly want to go shopping. Not for pleasure or even out of necessity, but from a need to hear voices, to feel bodies moving around me. I stay in the shop for a long time. I watch the people in the aisles, between the boxes of pudding and dog food. I fill up my basket with canned food that I choose randomly, sometimes because I like the colours of the labels. I would have stayed to watch people longer, but, after a while, I'm afraid I'll be noticed. So I go to the cash register. From there, I see Vera through a window in a little room having lunch with some other women. I hear them laughing, their voices, then Vera turns towards me and stands up. I would prefer it be someone else, it would be an opportunity to talk to someone new. Vera rings me up and I leave. It starts to rain.

When I get home I put my things away and wipe the dishes. They're almost dry, but, that's OK, it gives me something to do. And then he comes in, like a cat. It's his breath that I sense first. His breath and his fingers. I lean backwards so he can hold me. I know he'll catch me. I feel his hand open my lips and travel across my face. Black, white, colour. The sink starts to sparkle, the table, the chairs. The entire room puts on its party clothes and the dance begins. It's crazy, a man, when you think about it, the disturbance he creates.

'On Sunday, after church, I hiked up the volcano. I put your letter in a box that I hid between two lava stones. No one will ever find it. Your letter is beautiful. I would never be able to write you things like that.'

Saul is silent for a moment and looks out the window.

'When I got back from the volcano, Bonnie was waiting for me. She asked me to follow her into the kitchen. Her Bible was on the table. "Put your hand on it, and swear that nothing happened." I swore,' Saul simply said.

He smiled.

'We could arrange to meet,' I told him. 'Every other day, at the same time?'

Saul doesn't speak. Then he takes my hand and looks steadily into my eyes.

'You know, Ida, time here doesn't flow like clockwork. You're used to preparing, making plans, being organized, but here, you can't foresee things, you saw that on Bird Island. We never know what the day holds in store: fishing, unloading, a day of hunting at the Caves, a storm, the fields. It's the wind that decides, Ida. We move along with it, like the clouds hanging in the air.'

Then Saul stops talking and lets his head fall into his hands.

'I'd like to see you, too. Every day, at the same time, but we're too close. Can you understand? We live too close to each other.'

While he's talking, Saul squeezes my wrist, so strongly that I'm afraid he's going to break it. Then he suddenly lets go.

'I'll make a plan, you'll see, I'll make a plan, I promise, Ida.'

Saul kisses me deeply, then puts a life jacket he has been wearing onto one of the kitchen chairs.

'I slipped out of work. I told the guys I was going to return Mike's life jacket to him. I have to go now, they must have finished loading the tractor; we're going to replace the fences that the bloody wind took down yesterday at Runaway Beach.'

Saul looks outside to make sure the coast is clear, then leaves, his hands in his pockets, as if nothing had happened.

That's it. The fireworks stop, the party is over, everyone goes home. I'm bleeding. My lip is bleeding. Saul must have bitten it. Or maybe I did when I sunk down on the sofa. I don't know.

I get up, go to the window and lean my forearm on the steamed pane. A fly lands on the glass and slowly gravitates around my hand. It's odd, it leaves no trace. I wonder how it holds on.

11th day.

I have never known how to separate. Not words from life, not images from objects. Never known whether a portrait of a man or a fictional character seemed more real to me.

So, you who are here, too far to be so close, you who haunt my nights and destroy my bearings, of you I have only words and the colour of my work to rekindle a bit of the breath that, when the evening comes, heats my skin.

Eleven o'clock. The sound of Betty's brisk steps clacking on the tiles in the entryway. The neighbour woman puts the daily tub of peeled potatoes down in the sink. Sometimes, the old woman also wipes the dishes and sweeps up so Mike and Vera will return from work to a clean house.

But today, before leaving, Betty slips her head through the open doorway to the living room where I usually read in the morning. She stays there for a long moment just looking at me, not saying anything.

'Would you like to come over to knit? I could teach you how to make socks. You know, once you know how to make a heel, it's not very complicated.'

Her invitation is touching. Betty is nice. It must be obvious that I'm getting bored.

'Tomorrow, at 3.30, will that do you?'

I raise my head to respond, but too late, Betty is gone.

Without thinking, I put down my book, lace up my sneakers and go down the sunken path that separates the house from the store. I'm delighted: for the first time, I have a real reason to go there! At the shop I buy two skeins of yarn. One orange, the other blue, not too big, rather thin yarn, so I will soon need to return to buy more.

Then I go down to the port. Several boats are lined up on the shoreline, patiently waiting for the next fishing day. I look for number 8, Mike and Saul's boat. Saul described it to me at length on Bird Island. 'The sturdiest, the fastest, the easiest to handle,' he said. I really liked when he talked to me; the roundness of the words, his way of composing silences, the veil of mist that covered his voice. I sit down at the end of the jetty, my feet hanging freely, and stay there for some time, watching the never-ending ballet of albatrosses and black puffins flying above the waves. The sea is strange, seemingly always immutable, and yet never the same.

As I'm going back to the village, a raspy voice makes me jump:

'Unbelievable! Don't Frenchies know it bad luck to walk under ladders?'

I look up and, blinded by the sun, make out a short man, paint brush in his hand, suspended in the sky.

'I'm sorry, I was thinking of something else, and, with the sun . . .'

Without letting me finish, the man bursts out laughing:

'No worries, m'dear, I'm jestin' wit ya! Ya know, back home in Bulgaria, they even say that if ya sew a dress without taking it off it's bad luck, and ya can't never take the last portion of food. Load of horse shit, if ya ask me! Anyways, I'm outta paint. Come on, let me buy ya a drink?'

The stocky little man climbs down from the ladder and holds out an energetic hand.

'I'm Andreï, the poor mechanic who spends his life repairing old vats in the cannery. And I'm tellin' ya, despite what ya see, it ain't work that's lackin' here!'

'Ida. A pleasure,' I say, feeling my hand disappear in his.

Andreï puts his brush in a whitish liquid and gestures for me to follow but no sooner do we cross the threshold of his house than a thick smell of something burning fills our noses.

'The petrels!' shouts Andreï, holding his head. 'This mornin', Saul brought me the birds and I forgot 'em in the oven! I can't believe it! Not possible!'

A flood of I guess Bulgarian cursing comes out of the mouth of the sixty-something man who turns off the gas, takes the carbonized pot out of the oven, and opens the windows.

'OK, I take care of that later. Some brandy? That's what we come for, eh!'

I nod, happy to be here with this unknown person, despite the terrible stench of charred bird that fills the room.

We sit down at a plastic table covered with an oilcloth. Andreï sees the two skeins of yarn sticking out of my bag.

'What you gonna to do with that?'

'Knit some socks,' I say shyly. 'Betty offered to teach me.'

'Ah, I see!' Andreï says, amused. 'I hope you not plannin' on givin' 'em as gift, because they gonna stink like scorched petrel!'

No sooner has he finished talking than the Bulgarian bursts out laughing, his cheer echoing in the room. We laugh for a long time, leaning back in our chairs, like two teenagers, then Andreï catches his breath:

'Anyways, they's not much else to do here. When my wife come last year, she so bored she start knittin'. And she must be really bored, cause in forty years of life together, it first time I see her with needles in hands! After few days, Vera come ask her if she want to cut hair, they know she hair-cutter. I tell them. You bet! Next day, whole island line up in front of house, even in yard, imagine! Hair everywhere, you can't walk. Elena can't believe. But, you say, at least she not bored no more. The women bring eggs, socks, potatoes. Enough for whole year!'

Andreï pours us some more brandy.

'Last week, I come on *Austral* with Belgian reporter. I think he come here for story. I tell him he can go see you. Belgium and France, they alike, no? Both speaking French, you should have many things to tell each other. But he not stay long, until next boat, I think.'

'But how did you know I was on the island?'

Another great burst of laughter again makes his little moustache tremble.

'You, it clear you really not from these parts! Everyone know everything here, m'dear. Eyes everywhere! Well, not long ago, I go for walk near potato fields, over there, near Hottentot Gulch, and dog bites me. Rare here, but can happen. There was nobody around me, not a motorbike, not car, nothing. Well, next day at cannery, everybody knows. You tell me. But I no care, I got nothin' to hide.'

I lower my eyes and swallow a final swig of brandy, unsure of what I should make of what Andreï said. The mechanic is about to serve me again, but it's starting to get dark.

'Thank you, Andreï, but I have to get back, I don't want Vera and Mike waiting with dinner for me.'

'Go ahead,' he says, smiling. 'But we laugh good, you gotta come back!'

Just as I'm going into the house the phone rings. It's Nadia, the administrator's secretary.

'I've just received a message from Léon,' she tells me, as if she knows him. 'He's cancelled his ticket on the next boat.'

There was something cold, a tone of reproach in her voice. I hang up and burst into tears.

14th day.
You're not coming, Léon. So you're not coming.
Forgive me, forgive me, Léon. It's probably for the best.

Three-thirty. I go down the little path that leads from Betty's gate to her front door. She opens the door and invites me to follow her. Her house is a grotto, a nest, a magical temple decorated with glass cabinets populated with knickknacks, fishing trophies and family photos.

The old woman asks me to sit down, pours some tea, and without transition, begins the lesson. 'Right side, wrong side, stitches, rows, heel,' the words file by; I take out my notebook and try to capture them before picking up my needles and jumping into the water. I love touching the wool, it's soft, it reminds me of petrel down.

The afternoon goes by calmly, warmed by the sweetness of the tea and Betty's voice as she counts, casting on the stitches one by one to get me going. It does me good to be here, in this warm and protective oasis, this island on the island that goes against the laws of space and time. Then the gate creaks and the two dogs stand up. A short, round man takes off his boots and greets us.

'So, all is well, the socks are ready?' he says, smiling, 'Because you're going to have to make mountains of them for this weekend!'

I look up from my work, bewildered.

'Mike didn't tell you? This weekend it's Ratting Day!' Betty's husband informs me, taking a Black Label out of the fridge, as if he were hoping the beer would give him the energy needed to continue with what he was saying. 'Ratting Day is the event of the island! We're even paid by the government to go hunting, pretty good, eh? The goal is to capture as many rat tails as possible in one day. You'll see, it's great fun,' says Ray, before swallowing a big mouthful of the brown liquid.

While he's talking, I imagine hundreds of rodent bodies piled up along the road. Ray would happily go on, but Betty is looking at the clock.

I understand it's time for me to leave. I stand up, gather up my skeins and thank the couple for having me.

21st day.

I would like a confidant, a friend, a teammate. She could be called LÉONE.

Léone is lovely. Both wild and completely familiar.

The moon is still floating above the volcano when I hear voices coming from the dining room. It must be five o'clock, five-thirty at the most. I get up, get dressed and go into the hallway, guided by the fluorescent light. Saul and Mike are leaning their elbows on the kitchen island opposite Vera who, her hair still dishevelled, is mechanically filling their glasses with gin which the two buddies drink down in one gulp, as if to better punctuate what they're saying. Saul turns around and says hello with a nod of his head. I know he's happy to see me, maybe he even came just for that. Then, suddenly, the gong rings and everything gets underway: the windows of the houses light up, voices rise from the village and motors start humming, in an instant transforming the little road into an express lane. Today is Ratting Day! A few seconds later, the whole team arrives. I recognize Ben, Mike's nephew, Oliver, Bill and Jimmy. I'm happy to see Jimmy. I haven't seen him since we got back from Bird Island.

And, still blanketed in darkness, the day begins. Dogs are running around, overexcited by the hunt and the dancing of torch beams that navigate the ground like little beacons. You can sense the elation in people's hearts, hear the energy in their voices. Then, suddenly, Franky stops and begins to bark, starts running and is joined by two border collies. The men hurry behind them and work together to lift up a huge block of stone while Mike and Jimmy poke the ground, armed with their crowbars and other tools. As the men continue digging, the high-pitched sounds of the rats get closer, then the block rolls away and the dogs attack the nest, catching the fleeing rodents. Ben and Jimmy run to the dogs and extract the little writhing and squeaking animals from their mouths, then bang the rats' heads against a stone and cut off their tails. The men and the dogs are overjoyed. I just watch. The deaths don't disturb me.

Gradually, the first rays of sun awaken the colours in the fields. We can see the grey of the road, the brown of the stones and the green of the hills, wrapped by the blue bubble of the sky and the sea, unseparated by a horizon. Between each catch, all day long, we sit down on the grass and empty one by one the bottles of gin, sherry and beer that Ben, a perfect walking drink cart, takes out of his sack. With each new capture, old Bill proudly counts the number of tails that have been cut off and compares the number to that of the year before. Bill makes me laugh, his laid-back attitude, his happiness, the incandescence of his delight.

Back in the village, as night is falling, the community is gathered in front of the hospital where the island administrator, the veterinarian and the doctor are busy counting the rat tails collected by the teams. Saul is there, lurking in the shadows. He takes advantage of the hubbub to signal to me to follow him, and disappears into the darkness. A few minutes later, we're driving across the village in his Land Rover before turning onto the patches road. Around us, everything is black, only the yellow halo of the headlights that sweep the asphalt can be seen. Then Saul suddenly speeds up. He's drunk, completely drunk. I'm afraid a cow will cross the road, that a dog will appear, that the car will run off the road, but I don't say anything, I do nothing, probably reassured by the idea that, if the car goes off a cliff, I'll die with him. The Land Rover stops racing a few metres from the sand pile that blocks the road. Saul turns off the headlights, takes a bottle of whiskey from under his seat and turns on the radio. The music is so loud that it masks the sound of the wind banging against the windows and makes the car tremble.

Deep in the night
I'm looking for some fun
Deep in the night
I'm looking for some love
De-de-de-deep in the night
I'm looking for some fun
Deep in the night
I'm looking for some . . .

Saul holds the bottle out to me mechanically. I feel the alcohol going into my stomach, completely anesthetizing me. I feel empty, totally empty. Then nothing more. A black hole. My sketchbook is my only memory.

22nd day.
I write, I believe, pen in hand. I've drunk, drunk so much that I feel nothing, that I see nothing except the emptiness that dances and sways around me. I don't know anymore, the time, the space, the wind. Do you hear me, Léone? Léone, do you

hear me? Fucking life, fucking island, fucking rats, fucking echo that rings in my voice.

Suddenly it's very bright, like in films, I'm going down to a little beach next to the port. Franky, Mike and Vera's dog, is with me. Franky is funny, the way he turns his head when he watches the pebbles bouncing over the surface of the water. I open my eyes. Around me everything is white, just like after an accident. I can feel the ground and the grass on my neck.

It takes me three days to recover. Vera and Mike don't say a thing. I don't know what they know. I don't know what they don't know. And I don't know where Saul is or how he is. As usual. So I go out to draw. I sit down on the top of Hillpiece and take out my sketchbook. This morning, without paying attention, I open it in landscape format. And suddenly everything seems easier to me, more obvious, less compact; air rises up from the hills and the horizon appears.

Since then, every morning I return to Hillpiece and begin the same drawing again, realizing, day after day, just how much the immobility and monotony force me to enter inside the image, to look for each nuance, to dig into the matter and sound the masses.

I am out of blue chalk and the greens are running low. It's a shame, I should have foreseen it. So I draw in red, yellow, purple. It's funny to see the island like that, it makes it seem tropical, like a slightly exotic island.

5

And the rain, the silence, the clouds. Everything began again. Then you knocked and came in, without warning, on your little golden horse. We didn't speak. Not the time, not the place, not this time. Your hands took everything, razed everything, like your mouth between my legs, at that very place where ecstasy joins bliss. And you left to go back to your life. You rubbed my head and I closed my eyes, until I woke up.

And the days go by, time stretches out, like that tractor which, every morning, I hear coming from far away. It announces itself, warning, before inviting itself into the frame of my window only to leave it slowly; an extension tractor; a motor with three speeds: appearing, seen, extending.

And now the tractor has gone by.

This evening, Vera has put on a dress and a new cloth on the table. It has blue flowers on it. She has prepared lobster tails, the way I like, in the oven with a little butter and chopped parsley. Then we sit down at the table, choosing, for once, the kitchen table over the grey sofa and the television. Vera and Mike look at each other, solemn.

'Well, Mike and I would like to ask if you would agree to be godmother to our calf, the little white one that was born last week?'

At first I don't believe it. That they would ask me that. Me. Despite the silences, their detachment, their apparent indifference. And Saul? How can I agree without telling them? Maybe they know. But then, why ask me?

'We thought we'd call her Ida, like you. We really like "Ida". And then, that way, when you leave, you will always be here a bit, with us,' Vera continues, and I see her hand slide under the table and take that of her husband.

In front of us, the lobsters are steaming in the middle of the blue flowers. The tablecloth is beautiful. The arrangement of the design, the colour of the cornflowers. I don't know. I don't know anymore, torn between the fear of betrayal and happiness, huge, in accepting that honour.

'Yes, yes, I'd love to,' I say, raising my glass. 'Vive la vache! Vive Ida!'

We clink our glasses, smiling, then Vera serves us and no one speaks as we begin to eat.

'Ida, come on, Ida, come on.'

I imagine Vera's voice on milking days rising in the field and returning as an echo, sent back by the steep slopes of the volcano. The tone would be peremptory, almost authoritarian; that's how Vera talks to the cows. Maybe even Saul would hear. Who knows?

The meal over, Vera puts the rest of the lobster in Franky's dish and, like every evening, we settle down in front of the television. Mike takes off his slippers and Vera takes out her knitting; a scarf, red, with green patterns. Vera knits quickly, without even looking at the stitches that move, like a long caterpillar, between the wooden needles.

The film has just started when the phone starts ringing. Vera puts down her knitting, gets up, and answers.

'Ida, it's for you,' she tells me without reacting. I get up, surprised, and go to the phone. 'Saul is waiting for you in front of Little Green Hill. He's on his motorbike,' the unknown voice of a man tells me before hanging up.

I replace the phone on its base. In front of me, Vera and Mike are staring at the TV screen, motionless.

'I'm going to the bar. They need someone for the snooker team,' I say, not proudly.

Outside, thousands of stars pierce the bluish ocean of the night. I run down the road quickly in the direction of Hill-piece and the potato fields, climb over the iron bars and continue to Little Green Hill. There, you appear, coming out of nowhere on your iron bird. And it begins, everything begins again, like a beginning, like a story; we take off, we fly away, sucked in by the unconscious and voracious urgency to be two.

And the motor roars, covering the noise of the ocean. I am well, I feel well, I'm going, carried by the wind that stiffens my face and swims in my hair. I recognize every mound, every hill, every ravine, and this road, always this road, undulating and deserted, lighted by the wild and swollen flare of the moon.

Suddenly, the motorbike slows down. Saul stops and parks it behind a little house bedecked with sheet metal and wood. He takes off his helmet and looks at me, apologetic.

'I left as quickly as I could. So quickly that I forgot to bring the key to my cabin. I wanted you, you know, really wanted you. I'm so sorry, Ida.'

With a strong tug, Saul pulls on the door that reveals a tiny chamber.

We stay there, closed up in this square metre space. A hide-out, a kennel, a locked cage. But what does it matter? Already, the horizon slips and drops underground. No more sky or sea, no more high or low. We climb, heads backwards, we move the walls and raise the roof. My sight is blurry, my body in motion—with restriction. My pulse accelerates. Movements, too. 'Ida, Ida,' dull shouts, staccato breathing, excited gasps rise up in a mechanical rhythm and carry me off, entirely. And it rises, it grows, overwhelming the end point. No more time, no more space, just a line, long and continuous.

We stay there, not moving, depleted. Around us, the walls close in, the walls again become wood and the sea, in the distance, can be heard again. I'm doing fine, I'm doing fine. Outside, the moon is hiding behind the clouds.

And the bike starts up. The road, the volcano, the hills and the black grass, cut by the wind, thick, that sticks to our faces. Saul lets me off at the entrance to the village before disappearing. I walk, my body awake. I feel strong. Both strong and so light.

I see him immediately when I go into the Albatross Bar. A short man, all grey, leaning on the bar. Before I can even sit down, the journalist calls out to me, as if he was expecting me.

'So?' he asks, the way one asks for news from a close friend after a long trip.

That evening, I don't feel like talking. Not now, not in French. I want to keep the taste, the smell, the still-warm imprint of his kisses on my skin. I order a Black Label from Johanna.

'So?' the man says again, 'Isn't your experience here incredible? Six months. They told me you've been living on this isolated island, this lost bit of land on the far side of the world, for six months. It's amazing!' exclaims the man before taking a large swallow of beer without wiping off the foam sticking to his moustache. 'Do you realize we're in the most remote bar on the planet? Look at them, look at those people, this community which, against all odds, fights every day for its survival, braving the elements.'

I turn around. Behind me, Ray, Betty's husband, and Rod, his brother, are playing dominos on a low table. In the distance, the clashing of the snooker balls and the cries of the young people escape from the back of the bar. There are a lot of people today, more than other nights.

'My colleagues would have given anything to be in my shoes, as you can imagine! A space like this, an authentic bit of the world preserved from civilization. We are in the *isola*, my friend, the archetypical, the true, and the air that we're breathing is the purest in the world! Do you know that we're on the island where the most shipwrecks occur?'

The journalist continues, listing the dates, the records, the superlatives. I listen. I feel empty, completely empty. Is it his voice, the rhythm of his sentences or the horrible sensation of not having been able to see anything?

'What about you? What brought you here?'

His use of 'tu', his familiarity, surprises me; it's probably that so-called complicity that some travellers seek to create with others.

His question takes me by surprise. I don't know. I no longer know. I want to leave, I want to flee, to go through the door of the bar and go back to Saul. But I don't flee, I stay there, nailed to my chair, waiting for a divine voice to clear my memory.

'There was supposed to be two of us, but there was only one place left on the boat. So we tossed a coin, and I won.'

At that moment, Johanna rings the little bell hanging behind the counter, the signal that the bar will be closing soon. I quickly finish my beer, relieved at the idea of going home.

'Frédéric Franquelin,' says the man, holding out his hand. 'Here, I'll give you my card. The article should come out in December, for the Voyage supplement. The beer is on me,' he says with a wink.

Léone,

Have I separated from her? The one who, from over there, saw the island as a point for fleeing, a current of air. And now? Where am I? Who am I on the other side of the mirror?

Leave. With oneself, in spite of oneself, one's head in the clouds, tell oneself that beginning again is still possible. But

the island is there. Did you see it, Léone? The island is there,
and it does no good to run, when one brings oneself along.

It's the silence that awakens me, the silence and the memory,
sweet, of your spray on my skin. Outside, it's dark. I get up,
dress, and join Mike and Vera who are getting ready to leave.
Every evening, before going to bed, I ask them to knock on my
door and wake me up for the milking, but they have never done
it. I don't know why. We take the two buckets, the two potato
pails, put on our boots, turn on our torches and leave for the
Back Field where Suzy and Blacky are waiting for us. I would
like to stay there with Mike and Vera; I wish they wouldn't go
to work, not abandon me, not leave me alone to confront the
uniform and endless day that stretches out before me.

But it's no use: at eight o'clock the couple leaves for work.
I remain, emotionless, useless, watching the same days, the
same neighbours, the same cousins, the same sheep to shear, to
kill, to eat, to knit, the same cow to milk, to feed, to wean. The
islanders invent new recipes using the same ingredients, they
take new paths to always go to the same place, they transform
the 'no choice, we're eating potatoes' into 'I have the choice
between five kinds of different potatoes.' The choice stretches
out, time stretches out. Nothing, stretch out the nothing into
very little, then into a little, so it becomes a lot.

The stones look like walls closing in on me, a vise. She, she
watches, immobile, inflexible, perched on the top of the vol-
cano as if on a roost. She doesn't say a word, looking at the
body, my body, assailed by those torturing walls. Suave mari

magno. *What can I do in the face of her? She, the community, this safe, this cold room, this colossus with steel eyes that, from the top of its pinnacle, watches me without blinking to feed the conversations and chitchat of Saturday night.*

This morning, Saul calls. Next Saturday his wife is planning a party for her fortieth birthday. 'She's inviting the entire island, except you,' he tells me. 'But don't worry, I've got a plan. And believe me, you'll have a lovely evening.' He seems ill at ease, even sad, I can hear it in his voice. Then Saul hangs up. He must be at work. I expect him to come over, but no one comes except Betty to leave her tub of potatoes in the sink. Then Betty leaves and I feel like I can't breathe. I pick up a pencil, my sketchbook, and I go out to draw.

This morning, a boat went by in the distance. A container ship, I think. I used Mike's binoculars, from the kitchen cupboard, and I followed the ship, until it disappeared. In the evening, at the bar, everyone talked about it. Some said they had recognized a Maltese flag. Others, Sri Lankan.

And you, Saul, where were you? You weren't there.

And the weekend comes with its share of tasks and rituals. I like the weekend, the time goes by more quickly, Mike and Vera are there. I follow them around everywhere, whenever I can, like their third dog. We go to replace the flowers on the graves in the little cemetery, between the cliffs and the school, we feed the cows, make pizzas for birthdays. Sometimes, on Saturday, Mike and Will, Saul and Vera's nephew, bring me with them to Runaway Beach. That's where they practice rifle shooting on a cow skull fixed to a fence. Before we go, we always stop by Jake's, the island's policeman. He offers us something to drink and gives the guys their boxes of shells, then I go sit with the dogs in the back of the pick-up, I draw the hills and the road that pass behind us. I'm happy.

A short time ago we started to take turns cooking. This evening it's my turn. I make coq au vin with the chicken Mike killed yesterday and with the 'grape juice' I bought at the shop. For dessert I make a floating island. 'Floating island,' I say as I bring the dish out. Mike and Vera don't seem to understand, so I explain 'the yellow cream is the sea and the beaten egg white is the island.' We look at each other and laugh. I never did find out if they had understood.

When the meal is over, Vera puts on a dress, and Mike, his black slacks. They take beer, a bottle of brandy and the red scarf with green patterns that Vera wrapped up for Bonnie.

They leave right after the meal, probably uncomfortable, too, that Bonnie hadn't invited me to her party. I watch them walk away, leaning on the gate, Vera holding on to Mike so she won't slip in her high heels.

I don't even have time to clean up; no sooner has the couple left when Will, Saul's nephew, knocks on the door.

'Hi,' he says.

I don't know if he has come on Saul's behalf, or if he is just stopping by. He must sense my question, because, just then, he plunges his hand into his pocket and rattles the keys to his uncle's pick-up.

'Shall we go?'

I put on my polar fleece, pick up a pencil, my sketchbook, and follow Will who gets behind the wheel. The car starts up and so does the radio, at full blast. We leave the village. The road unfolds in front of us, drowning in the night, it smells like dog, wet dog and cold tobacco. Will opens the window and lights a cigarette. I see his bony cheeks, his military haircut, his two large blue eyes. Will is handsome. He looks like Saul. A little. When we arrive at the fields, Will turns right and parks in front of the cabin. I recognize the wood, the stainless steel, the door of the little cabin which, a few weeks earlier, had been the welcome scene of our lovemaking.

Will takes a key out of his pocket, yanks on the outer door and opens the door to the inner room. He puts a large bag down on the cement floor, lights a gas lamp and takes out an old radio from under one of the camp beds. His movements are fluid, it looks like he's dancing. Then the pop music begins to play, like in the car on Bird Island, like Saturday at home.

'Don't worry, everyone is at the birthday party, no one will hear.'

I look at Will. I smile. Already, I had forgotten: Vera, the party, Saul, Bonnie, that other world two kilometres away.

Will takes two large white eggs out of his bag, and places them carefully on the Formica table. He turns on the hot plate, takes a large pan from a wooden crate and empties what remains of a bottle of petrel oil into the pan. The fat jumps and sizzles like little fireworks. Then Will breaks the two large eggs, which spread in the bottom of the pan until they cover it completely.

'Don't know how Saul managed to keep them, penguin eggs are rare this time of year. He must have hidden them, because there are a lot of folks who would be interested. When my sister was small, she thought that rockhopper eggs were little jellyfish, because of the whites. See, even when they're cooked they stay transparent,' says Will, stirring the pool of mucus that covers the pan with the back of his fork.

We eat. I savour the heat of the liquid, the fishy aftertaste, the vitreous gelatine that I let melt on my tongue, and the enormous yolk that you're supposed to swallow all at once, laughing.

When the meal is done, Will turns off the lamp and lights a candle that he puts between the two camp beds. We lie down and smoke a cigarette. The music has stopped. Outside, the wood creaks and the steel vibrates under the wind.

'What's it like over there?' Will asks me, exhaling a large puff of smoke.

'Where, over there?'

'Where you live, on the mainland!'

'You've never been?

'Yes, once, to do a diving training course. It was at False Bay, near Cape Town.'

'Did you like it?'

'Yeah, I think. Actually, I didn't really see much. We stayed at a camp and, in the evening, we went to a bar. That's where I got my tattoo.'

Will raises the sleeve of his fleece. A large tribal motif with the number 6 above it surrounds his biceps.

'It's the number of my boat,' Will tells me, anticipating my question. 'It's the sturdiest and the most sea-worthy!'

I smile. On Bird Island, Saul had told me exactly the same thing about his boat. We stay silent for a long time, lying on the two camp beds.

'Before leaving for South Africa, I thought that Europe and the Cape were next to each other. When you leave here, everything seems so close!'

Will looks at me and smiles, obviously embarrassed at having confessed such a thing to me. I sit up on the bed and take out my sketchbook.

'There must be some really pretty girls on the mainland!'

'I don't know. I think there's a bit of everything, like everywhere. What do you do for work here?'

'Department of public works. When I got out of school, I first did an internship at the post office, but I got tired of it: I spent my time licking stamps and, at the end of the day, my tongue was dried out. And I also fish for the cannery, like everyone, right? Recently, the company told us to keep the octopuses, too, it seems those are sold in Japan,' he says with a doubtful look, taking a long draw of his cigarette. 'What about you? What do you do for a job?'

'I draw. I'm an illustrator.'

Will starts laughing.

'I'm really bad at that sort of thing, I remember, I always got bad grades in drawing. One day, with the class, we went down to Big Sandy Gulch to draw the cows. Miss Mary told us that the farther away the cows were, the smaller you had to draw them, "to give depth," but the cows were all the same size!' Will puts out his cigarette in a beer cap and swallows a mouthful of brandy. 'You need to explain, I still don't understand.'

We lay on the cots, our gazes suspended on the drywall slabs of the ceiling.

'Thanks, Will. It's nice of you to spend the evening with me. I imagine you had better things to do.'

Will turns his head towards me and smiles.

'No, I like this. And, I really owe Saul one. I shouldn't tell you this, but, you know, Saul loves you, Ida.'

Will turns off the lamp. I slip into my sleeping bag and close my eyes. Outside the wind has calmed down; we hear the sound of the waves, very close, and the cries of the night-birds fading into the dark.

Tomorrow, Léone, the boat arrives. Saul told me this morning after he surprised me by slipping under my covers. He is waiting for some wire to repair the fences and a replacement part for his motorbike.

I run down the path. Already, dozens of curious onlookers are crowding the quay, seated on the edge as if they're at the theatre. Everyone is watching the parade of barges and the motorized platform that moves between the port and the icebreaker anchored offshore. Next to me, Meg and Nadia,

Mike's two sisters, say the names of the passengers one by one as they disembark.

'The *Spire* wants to leave asap right after it unloads, because a good south-western is suppos'd to arrive tonight,' Andreï tells me, sitting down next to me. 'It's headin' for another island, farther south, to pick up a crew of scientists for winter. In three weeks, it come back here before headin' back to Cape. Afterwards, we be at peace again for few more months,' the chief mechanic says to me, laughing.

We stay for a long time watching the ballet of barges that, one by one, let off little groups of passengers, around whom islanders gather, greeting them warmly.

'Hey, look, there's the most beautiful!' Andreï says, pointing at Ray and Betty who are walking quickly to meet their daughter and their grandson who have just reached land. It's true, they're in their Sunday best for the occasion; Betty is wearing a necklace and a long, blue sweater. Ray has replaced his boots for a pair of loafers. Betty was overjoyed at the idea of seeing them. 'It's been such a long time since my daughter has been here, she lives in England,' she told me yesterday, after setting down her basin of potatoes in the sink.

The show over, I go back up to the house. The lines of chicks, the rows of little gardens, the mounds of tussocks: everything reminds me of that morning a hundred years ago when, I, myself, set foot on the island for the first time.

At the house, I find the garage transformed into a true butcher shop; hanging from the ceiling, an imposing cow carcase is dancing in the middle of a group of men who are busy cutting up the animal. The women are standing in the garden, grouped around a huge vat, a thick cloud of steam escaping out of it. Nadia, Mike's sister, comes up to me and holds out a knife.

'All's fair in love and war,' she says, handing me a piece of stomach whitened by the hot water.

I put down my sketchbook, roll up my sleeves and join the group. The offal, the intestines, the heat on one's skin, I remember the happy team we formed on Bird Island, crouched on the rocks, cutting up the petrels and separating the fat from the skin.

Around me, the women are laughing. Vera, too. She seems more at ease when the men aren't around, and proves more than capable as head of the operation. I watch her sort, organize, wash and diligently give orders to put the tripe into bags to freeze it when it's clean.

When the work is done, we go back in the house to warm up. Ben, Mike's nephew, turns on the hi-fi and invites Nadia to dance, while Vera and Mike, attentive hosts, fill everyone's glasses with brandy, sherry, whiskey or beer. Gradually, a sweet happiness suffuses the room. Assisted by the alcohol, tongues loosen, hands wander, stretching the limits of the forbidden. The older folks slouch in the armchairs, leaving room for the younger ones who, tipsy from the drinking, joke and laugh loudly. Suddenly, the legendary hit by the Scorpions rings out in the room. Vera sets her glass down hard on the table, and gives a piercing shout. She goes up to her audience, tunes her imaginary guitar and begins to play wildly. Everyone is quiet and watches her, except Mike who, his nose planted in his beer, is snoring on the sofa. And the music gets louder, intensified by the heady lamentations of the guitars. Vera does a spin around the floor, letting her hand dance on the invisible instrument.

> *Is there really no chance*
> *To start once again?*
> *I'm still loving you.*

She screams and prances around while waving her guitar, then she stiffens all of a sudden and stands in front of me. She stares at me right in the eyes until, unable to hold her gaze, I feel my head lowering. Vera remains standing, motionless, for a long time, just looking at me. Then she moves away and falls backward.

The next morning, Betty calls to cancel the knitting lesson.

'It's not a good day to come,' she told me. 'Anyway, today, the Albatross Bar and the shop are closed; with the flu, everything is closed! Every time it's the same, those nasty tourists bring us death. They'll be leaving in three weeks, but us, it takes us months to recover.' Poor Betty. She must feel terrible being sick when her daughter is there.

So I take my sketchbook, my pencils, and I walk without really knowing where I'm headed. I end up at Andreï's house. He is there, in his kitchen, busy preparing a meat soup with squash and potatoes.

When he sees me, Andreï sets two glasses on the oilcloth, brings his vegetables to the table, and continues to peel them.

'It seems everyone is sick,' I say, pensive.

'Oh, you know, it not surprising. Every time icebreaker comes, the same thing. Not lots of people come here, so, when there are some, it's Berezina.'

'Even the Albatross Bar is closed.'

'Yes, well that, it's a bad for a good, it make them drink less. Hey, you wanna hear some music?'

I get up and turn on the hi-fi. A languorous chant flows out of the speakers and softly rises up in the room. We sit for a long time, listening to the sound of the brass and the tambourines. Then Andreï puts his knife on the table and looks straight at me.

'It not my business, Ida, but I tell you things like I think, because, if I not do it, here, no one tell you anything. You remember, I tell you story of dog who bite me in the patches, I think no one see us, but next day, everyone knows. Here, walls have ears, everything is known. Us, we arrive, all good, all new, as if nothing wrong, but, believe me, it very fragile, Ida, a community, and soon everything all messed up.' Andreï stops for a moment. He stands up, takes a bottle of vodka from the fridge and fills our glasses. 'You leave, but them, they stay, all their life, with their past, their stories, their bitterness, their frustration, their happiness, too. In beginning, I, like you, didn't understand this strange switch between calm and storm, those tiny rituals, those dead times that seem endless when everyone look at each other for hours in whites of eyes as if time was eternal, and then suddenly, bam! storm arrives, boat leaves, wind turns, fishing starts, a passing ship explodes at sea, and nothing is like before. Must be both on alert, ready to go, to jump into first boat to help while watching life go by, never forcing anything. You see, all that, if you not born here, it far from certain!' Andreï finishes his glass and picks up his knife and finishes peeling his vegetables. 'Me, I survive because before setting foot here, for twenty years, I on boat. This island, for me, is like boat and my house, well, the one the cannery plant gave me, is like my cabin: I come home, I leave, but the rest, I not home, I no worry about it.' Andreï sets down his knife and looks at me again. 'In three weeks, the *Spire* returns before going back to Cape. I think there must be places on board. If I am you, I think about it.'

I don't say anything, not even goodbye, not even thank you. I leave, like a current of air.

On the path, I run into Will who is going fishing.

'Come on, get in,' he says.

Will knows everything. No need to talk. We leave the village and go to Runaway Beach. After we park, we take a pack of beer, a box of hooks and a piece of octopus for the lures from the trunk, and we settle down on the rocks. In two hours, we catch eighteen five fingers.

Léone,

The boat left day before yesterday, in the night. It will return in three weeks. Three weeks.

Time seems short to me, for the first time.

This morning, I visit Nadia at the administrative offices. The young woman has me sit down in her room, between a portrait of the Duke of Edinburgh and one of Queen Elizabeth.

'There are three places left on the *Spire*, reserved for medical emergencies. Shall I reserve one for you?' Nadia raises her voice to cover the sound of the coughing that comes out of the adjacent offices. She doesn't look that well, either, her eyes are swollen and her neck is wrapped in a thick wool scarf.

'Yes,' I answer, joylessly, then I get up and leave. I don't want to talk.

It's time, Léone, but I'm writing to you all the same. For better or worse. I don't know, but I'm leaving, it's decided. Are you coming Léone? I'll bring you with me.

Just as I shut my notebook, Saul appears, running, drenched in sweat. He opens the front door and runs to me.

'They told me you're leaving. Is that true, Ida?'

Saul looks at me, silently imploring me to speak.

'Yes,' I say, my voice crushed with sadness.

Saul raises his eyes. I watch him looking at my face for a long time. He smiles.

'Yesterday, the doctor set up an exam for me at the Somerset Hospital in Cape Town. I'll take the *Meridian* a few days after the *Spire* leaves. It recently postponed its arrival because of mechanical issues. We'll meet over there. Is that OK?'

I didn't have to beg, Léone, didn't have to cry. I didn't have to write that I'm leaving and he's crying. Saul will join me. There, on land. Saul will join me.

SAUL AND IDA

The days fly by, faster than I could have imagined. Each day, I pursue my pilgrimage: Hillpiece, Runaway Beach, Hottentot Gulch, the potato fields, the cows, the wind, the multicoloured cottages; I draw the way one hastily gathers up photos of loved ones before a long trip.

Yesterday, I finished my second pair of socks. They are pink with blue heels. I gave the two pairs to Mike and Vera when I told them I was leaving. They seemed happy, well, they didn't say anything in particular.

Day after day, I fill my suitcase with cans of deodorant, cups, key rings with an effigy of the island and pairs of socks that, every evening, Mike's and Vera's friends and family come to kindly give me. Andreï came, too. He brought me a photo of him on the *Elena*, his sailboat back in Bulgaria. Will gave me a sweater that his mother knit with wool from the sheep that he sheared the year before. It is beautiful, white, with long cables that run down the back.

And my last evening arrives. After an excellent stuffed mutton prepared by Vera, we set off for the hall. A dozen couples, grouped in the darkness, dance to the rhythm of the pop hits pouring out of enormous speakers. Rihanna, Kylie Minogue, Kesha, Jay Sean, Flo Rida, Sean Kingston, and between each song, I watch the ritual of men who cross the room to choose their partner and invite her to dance. Everyone is there: Will, Betty, Ray, Jimmy, Ben, Andreï, Nadia, and Frédéric, the Belgian journalist who, a perfect gentleman, invites a different woman for each new dance.

Gradually, the women shed layers, revealing their lace and their low-cut tops. The teenagers constantly move between the hall and the Albatross Bar.

I stay in the hall until the room empties, until the teenagers turn on the lights, until they pick up all the bottles and turn off the music. I'm tired from drinking too much, dancing, watching for Saul who didn't come. A pity. I would have liked him to come, I would have liked to watch him, one last time, swaying on the dance floor and dancing with his friends.

Before going to bed, I make a detour to Saul's house and I stand there, leaning on his garage, watching the television screen flickering through the curtains of their bedroom. I imagine him asleep. What is he dreaming about? What could he be dreaming about?

Outside, it's raining, Léone, tears flow out of the clouds, like in storms, like before a shipwreck. It's raining and you, you sleep, rocked by the flood of images that radiate in your room and fly off in the dark.

The helicopter grazes the roofs of the houses and pursues its dance between the Back Field and the *Spire* that is anchored offshore. Mike puts my suitcase in the back of the pick-up and turns on the engine. With my throat tight, I watch the little walls, the road, the mounds of tussocks, the coloured roofs of the houses pass by, and the Back Field, transformed, for a few hours, into a vast landing field.

Saul is there, next to Bonnie, drowned in the crowd grouped behind the stone walls that surround the pasture. Mike opens the door of the car and gives me a quick hug before disappearing into the group that is milling around us. Will runs up and gives me a hug while a long line of people forms in front of me. We hug, we squeeze, we think 'adieu,' but everyone says 'au revoir'.

Then I get in, I leave, I rise up in the air without taking my eyes off the bouquet of hands reaching up in the sky.

We fly over Hillpiece, Runaway Beach, Hottentot Gulch, the potato fields, the cows the wind, the multicoloured cottages and an island, a very little island, filled with birds and encircled by spray.

I would have liked to tell them, Léone. Let the words fly out. To 'them,' to 'them', to those who welcomed me, to those who housed me.

I would have liked to tell them, Léone. Those unthinkable words, those impossible things.

I would have liked to, but I didn't know how.

EPILOGUE

They arranged to meet at the Garden Centre in Vredehoek, in the middle of the snack and clothing shops. His gait was uncertain, his gaze hesitant; he looked like a frightened deer, lost in the middle of the rows of shop windows and escalators.

They went to the sea. The taxi drove along the coast to the promenade at Sea Point. The sound of the waves, the rocks, the departing boats, she told herself he would like it. They walked for a long time on the ridge, protected from the sun by the shade of the palm trees. He didn't dare touch her, like that, out in the open; to do like the couples that were walking in front of them holding hands, in front of everyone.

They ordered two bags of popcorn that a man was selling out of a small white truck before sitting down, in front of the sea, to nibble on the puffed corn, like two teenagers. Below, a man was throwing a stick for his border collie. He watched the scene like a professional: 'He shouldn't talk to him like that. It's all over—in a few months, it's the dog who will be master.'

She put her hand on his shoulder and let it slide along his back. He turned to her and looked at her. Her eyes, her mouth, her skin. He wouldn't forget anything, ever. Then they continued to walk. Too many things to say, to talk. Too many things to keep silent. And day fell. He took advantage of the dark to take her hand. She didn't say anything, she smiled without taking her eyes off the twinkles of light that were coming on in the distance.

In the taxi going back, despite the heat, she began to shiver. Her mouth, her arms, then her entire body. He took her hand and put his head on her shoulder.

Then the taxi stopped. He took her in his arms and simply said: 'It's not the end of the world.'

She thought it was.

Acknowledgements

I wish to thank Jacques Leenhardt, without whom this book would not exist.

Grazie di cuore a Nicola, il signore delle scatole.

Thank you to Solène, Anne-Claire and Lili.

C. B.